by Dixie Browning

Silhouette Desire has something very special for you—*The Passionate G-Man* by Dixie Browning, book one of her new miniseries, THE LAWLESS HEIRS.

In *The Passionate G-Man*, irresistibly sexy secret agent Daniel Lyon Lawless has a simple mission—to expose the operative who double-crossed him. But he has a hard time keeping his mind *on* the job and *off* the beautiful woman by his side when he gets stranded with Jasmine Clancy!

Be sure to look for the second book of THE LAWLESS HEIRS miniseries, tycoon H. R. Lawless's story, available in November from Silhouette's new 12-book promotional series, WORLD'S MOST ELIGIBLE BACHELORS.

THE LAWLESS HEIRS: A surprise will unites the Lawless family—and leads them to love!

Dear Reader,

MEN! This month Silhouette Desire goes man-crazy with six of the sexiest, heart-stopping hunks ever to come alive on the pages of a romance novel.

Meet May's MAN OF THE MONTH, love-wary secret agent Daniel Lawless, in *The Passionate G-Man*, the first book in Dixie Browning's fabulous new miniseries, THE LAWLESS HEIRS. Metsy Hingle's gallant hero protects an independent lady in danger in the last book of the RIGHT BRIDE, WRONG GROOM series, *The Bodyguard and the Bridesmaid*. Little bitty Joeville, Montana, has more tall, dark and rugged ranchers than any other town west of the Mississippi. And Josh Malone has more sex appeal than all of 'em put together in *Last of the Joeville Lovers*, the third book in Anne Eames's MONTANA MALONES series.

In *The Notorious Groom*, Caroline Cross pairs the baddest boy ever to roam the streets of Kisscount with the town virgin in a steamy marriage of convenience. The hero of Barbara McCauley's *Seduction of the Reluctant Bride* is one purebred Texas cowboy fixin' to do some wife-wranglin'—this new groom isn't about to miss a sultry second of his very own wedding night. Yeehaw! Next, when a suddenly wealthy beauty meets the owner of the ranch next door, he's wearing nothing but a Stetson and a smile in Carol Grace's *The Heiress Inherits a Cowboy*.

Silhouette Desire brings you the kind of irresistible men who make your knees buckle, your stomach flutter, your heart melt…and your fingers turn the page. So enjoy our lineup of spectacular May men!

Regards,

Melissa Senate

Senior Editor
Silhouette Books

Please address questions and book requests to:
Silhouette Reader Service
U.S.: 3010 Walden Ave., P.O. Box 1325, Buffalo, NY 14269
Canadian: P.O. Box 609, Fort Erie, Ont. L2A 5X3

DIXIE BROWNING
THE PASSIONATE G-MAN

SILHOUETTE *Desire*®
Published by Silhouette Books
America's Publisher of Contemporary Romance

SILHOUETTE BOOKS

ISBN 0-373-76141-4

THE PASSIONATE G-MAN

Copyright © 1998 by Dixie Browning

Printed in U.S.A.

DIXIE BROWNING

celebrated her sixtieth book for Silhouette with the publication of *Stryker's Wife* in 1996. She has also written a number of historical romances with her sister under the name Bronwyn Williams. A charter member of Romance Writers of America and a member of Novelists, Inc., Browning has won numerous awards for her work. She divides her time between Winston-Salem and the Outer Banks of North Carolina.

One

Lyon hobbled away from the truck stop with as much haste and dignity as he could muster, leaving the waitress staring after him, her tired blue eyes filled with sympathy. By all rights she should have clobbered him. Instead, she'd taken one look at his stricken face, another at his cane, and started in with the, "Oh, you poor man" routine.

Levering himself into the driver's seat, he brushed a crumb of fried oyster off his sleeve and shifted until he found a position that was bearable. He'd been warned against driving at all, much less driving for hours at a stretch.

Needless to say, he'd ignored the warning.

Dammit, he'd tried to apologize to the woman. It wasn't her fault he'd been in the process of extracting himself from the cramped booth just as she passed by with two big seafood platters.

Lyon was no good with apologies. Never had been.

He'd wanted to help her clean up the mess, but he knew better than to try, so he'd done the next best thing. He'd crammed a fistful of bills in her apron pocket and got the hell out of there, red face, grease-stained shoulders and all.

At least, with the help of a back brace, a knee brace and a cane, he could do that much. Walk away. There was damned little he was good at anymore, but he'd always been good at walking away.

Five weeks ago he had walked away from an explosion that had killed two other agents and three civilians. Crawled away, actually, after being blown clear. Miraculously, he'd suffered only minor burns, but he'd been thrown against the side of the surveillance van, injuring his back and one knee.

At least he'd survived.

Five days ago he had walked away from the hospital. He'd had a choice of lying there taped up like a mummy, waiting either to mend or to croak from sheer boredom—or for the bad guys to find him and put a permanent end to his career—or get the hell out.

He'd got out. Walked away. Because if the bad guys hadn't got to him first, the boredom would've done him in.

Although there'd been a couple of nurses who'd done their best to relieve it. One, a sweet-faced, middle-aged woman, had joked about adopting him.

Another one had been more interested in seducing him.

He might even have considered it—the seduction— if only to prove to himself that he still had a few working body parts, but the last thing he needed was to get involved with a woman.

It had been Lyon's experience that men and women viewed sex from widely different perspectives. Women—at least the few he'd been involved with for any length of time—used sex the same way he used the tools of his trade. As a means of achieving an end.

To all but one or two of the women he'd known, sex was bait. The female of the species was programmed by nature to latch onto the richest mate available. His old man had drummed that lesson into his head before he'd cleaned out the cash drawer where he worked and disappeared, leaving behind a bitter wife and an angry twelve-year-old son.

Lyon hadn't learned much from his father, but he'd heard that little homily repeated too often ever to forget it.

Cautious by nature, he'd learned to be even more cautious, both in his work and in his relationships with women. Not all women were dishonest. Not all of them were looking for commitment, but enough of them were so that he didn't care to take chances.

To a man, sex was relief. A basic requirement, like food and water and a couple of hours sleep out of every twenty-four or thirty-six hours, conditions permitting. For a man in his position, it didn't pay to think beyond that.

Back on the highway, Lyon tuned to a country music station and set his mind on automatic. There were too many things it didn't pay to think about. Not yet. Not until he was fully recovered, had a few answers and was ready to go back and deal with them.

He spotted the patrol car in plenty of time to ease his speed back to a safe and legal seventy. Not that he was afraid of getting pulled over. His ID, if he cared to use it, would get him past any branch of law enforcement. It was more a matter of common sense.

A matter of survival.

Common sense told him that a man in his condition had no business being on the highway at all. A well-honed sense of survival—which, admittedly had taken a beaten lately—told him that driving like a bat out of Daytona wasn't particularly smart, either. Especially as he'd quit cold turkey taking painkillers and muscle relaxants three days ago. As a result, he was hurting. As a result of something else, although probably not the pills, he was jittery.

The smoky lost interest. Lyon breathed a sigh of relief. Near the Virginia-North Carolina border he pulled into the visitors' center, parked and scanned the immediate surroundings out of habit. It was called situation awareness.

He took his time getting out of the pickup, not that he had an option. By the time he'd done three slow laps around the parking area, his muscles had loosened up enough so that he barely limped, even without the cane.

Mind over matter. His body might have been screwed over pretty thoroughly, but his mind was still in first-class working order.

Although there'd been some argument over that when he'd signed himself out of the hospital.

Following the road map, he left the interstate at Roanoke Rapids and took an east-southeasterly course, using two lanes and what was euphemistically called "other roads." There was no deadline. He had three months before he had to make up his mind whether to put in for early retirement or go back on line.

At least where he was headed there wouldn't be any reporters. Or any drug-runners, terrorists, or survivalists, any one of which was bad enough. When the territories started overlapping, things got spooky.

And when there was a leak from somewhere in the chain of command, things got even spookier. The wrong people started dying.

"How'd you want your burger, hon? We can't fry 'em rare no more, gov'ment rules. We got sweet onions up from Georgia, though. A thick slice, and even shoe leather'd taste good."

Lyon ordered two burgers, well-done with extra onion, extra cheese and a quart of coffee. When the waitress leaned across in front of him to realign the salt and pepper shakers, offering him a front-row seat in her balcony if he was interested, he said, "To go, please. And could you give me directions to—"

"Any old where, darlin', you name it. You here for the huntin' or the fishin'? I could show you some real good places."

"Yeah, both," he muttered. *I'll just bet you could, sugar, and I'd probably enjoy them all, but not today, thanks.* "Could you point me in the direction of the nearest hardware store, supermarket and the local tax office?"

Jasmine was depressed. All the way across the country she'd been pumping up her expectations.

She'd managed to keep them high during the long drive from the airport to the nursing home, but there they'd collapsed like a wet soufflé.

Her grandmother didn't know her. Her only living relative, whom she hadn't seen since she'd moved with her mother from Oklahoma to California eighteen and a half years ago, didn't know her from Adam.

Make that Eve.

And the worst part of it was, Hattie Clancy wasn't interested in knowing her. She was sweet and polite and a little vague—well, a lot vague, actually—but Jasmine could tell right off that she was more interested in playing cards with her friends and watching her favorite soaps and game shows than she was in getting to know the granddaughter who had flown all the way from the West Coast to see her.

Jasmine told herself it was probably for the best. Why get attached to someone who lives thousands of miles away, someone who's old and might die—someone who's probably set in her ways and wouldn't be interested in moving to L.A., even if Jasmine could afford to move her there?

All the same, it would have been nice...

She shook off the sense of depression. It hadn't been a total waste. She'd met her only living relative, after all. Now when she sent snapshots and letters and greeting cards, she'd have a face to attach to the name and address she'd found among her father's papers after he'd died.

Having barely known the man before he turned up one day on her doorstep, sick and broke, she'd been surprised to learn that his mother—her own grandmother—was still living, much less living in North Carolina. She would have thought Oklahoma if she'd thought at all, because that's where her parents had parted company.

Jasmine had written to Hattie Clancy immediately. She hadn't heard back, but she'd continued to write. For an actress who was unemployed more often than not, she'd been too busy trying to pay off her father's medical bills, along with her own living expenses, to have much free time, but she'd made time to send cards and brief notes, and sometimes a clipping when she happened to land a part and her name was mentioned in a review.

Which was practically never.

To make ends meet she'd done a few commercials and taken a fill-in job in a dress shop. It paid minimum wage, plus a tiny discount on clothes she couldn't afford to buy anyway.

And now she'd spent money she didn't have to fly east to see a grandmother who didn't know her and didn't seem particularly interested in getting acquainted. She might as well have stayed home. It had been a total waste of time and money.

No, it hadn't. She'd earned herself a vacation. The last one had been—

Yes, well…that was another reason she'd needed to get away. Her last vacation had been with Eric. A week after they'd come back from Tahoe, Eric had started seeing her best friend. Jasmine had made excuses for him at first. She was good at that.

What was that popular song? *Cleopatra, Queen of Denial?*

Boy, was she ever. Her friends said she was easy-going. Laid-back. Which meant more or less the same thing—that she didn't blow her stack at the least little thing, which was a definite advantage in the dog-eat-dog world of acting.

All the same, she hadn't felt very laid-back when Cynthia had breezed into the shop one day last week and said, "Guess what! Eric and I are getting married. You've got to be our maid of honor, you've simply got to! After all, if you hadn't introduced us, it never would have happened."

Right. Smartest thing she ever did. Introduce the man she was in love with to her best friend, who was blond and beautiful and had a continuing, if minor, role in *Wilde's Children.*

"When?" she'd managed to ask. Actually, it had sounded more like a whine, but Cyn had been so wrapped up in her own euphoria she hadn't noticed.

"Valentine's Day. Isn't that just too, too perfect?"

Jasmine had agreed that it was just too, too perfect. And then she'd come up with the too-too perfect excuse. "Oh, but my grandmother—it's her seventy-ninth birthday. Actually, her birthday's on the fifteenth, but I promised to help her celebrate. You wouldn't want to wait until next year, would you?"

They couldn't possibly wait, and so Jasmine had been stuck with her excuse. She'd told herself it would be a lovely thing to do, to surprise her grandmother—her only living relative, unless her father had taken a few more secrets to the grave—and so she'd flown all the way across the country on a ticket she couldn't afford, and gone still deeper in debt renting a car to drive to the nursing home, which was hours away from the airport.

And now, here she was at loose ends for a whole week. She'd planned to stay near the nursing home, only there wasn't really any place to stay—at least no place she could afford. She'd asked for a weekly rate on her car, and planned to drive her grandmother around, just the two of them, and talk about her father and her grandfather, and any aunts or uncles and cousins she might have.

Family things. Things like, who else in the family had kinky maroon hair and legs that went all the way up to her armpits?

Things like who else in the family loved animals, hated insects and was allergic to cantaloups?

Things that would have taken her mind off the fact that Cyn and Eric were at this very moment honeymooning in Cancún.

Instead, she'd spent a day at the nursing home, looking at pictures of grandchildren of people she didn't even know, watching soaps and seeing a few people she did know, but not Cyn, thank goodness— and being largely ignored by her own grandmother.

She'd played cards with three lovely old ladies, gradually coming to realize that they weren't all playing with a full deck. She'd strolled around the grounds once the rain had let up, exclaiming over straggly little flowers and squishing through the mud to pick a bunch of red berries for one of the residents who admired them.

She'd had to battle great swags of Spanish moss and several thick, hairy vines to get to the things, but when her grandmother had asked for some, too, she had gladly waded into the jungle again to oblige her.

What else were granddaughters for?

Feeling lost, rootless, she'd woken up the next morning and considered her options. If she went back now—that's if she could even exchange her tickets—she'd have to pay the daily rate for her car instead of the cheaper weekly rate.

Of course, she would save on her motel bill, but money wasn't her only problem, or even her biggest one. Eric and Cynthia would be back on Friday. Cynthia would insist on giving her a detailed description of the honeymoon. Cynthia insisted on giving anyone who would listen a detailed description of her entire life. It was one of her charms—her breezy openness.

And Eric, blast his gorgeous hide, would gaze adoringly into his bride's eyes the way Jasmine had dreamed of his gazing into her own eyes, only he never had, and she'd probably throw up or something equally embarrassing.

Dammit, he *knew* she loved him! She hadn't even tried to hide it. They'd met thirteen and a half months ago at a New Year's Eve party and it had been one of those magical, magnetic moments that come once in a lifetime.

They had everything in common. They'd both grown up in the Midwest in single-parent households, but they'd been happy, comfortable households. They both believed in love at first sight, in fate. They both liked vinegar on their french fries.

The first time they'd gone away for a long weekend together, Jasmine had thought of it as a honeymoon. She'd been waiting ever since for a proposal, being just old-fashioned enough to believe it was the man's prerogative. Which was a hoot considering she was an actress who had lived in L.A. for nearly five years.

And then she'd made the fatal mistake of introducing Eric to Cynthia.

After driving aimlessly for hours, she pulled into a service station, filled her tank, hoping her credit card wasn't maxed out, and splurged on a candy bar and a diet cola. Savoring the unfamiliar aroma of nature in the raw mingled with diesel oil, she studied the map in search of anything of interest between where she was and the airport.

She'd had to ask the attendant where she was. It seemed she was somewhere in the vicinity of Frying Pan Landing, not too far from Gum Neck, smack dab in the middle of that part of the map labeled Eastern Dismal Swamp.

Dismal. If she'd been looking for something that suited her mood, she couldn't have found a better place.

"I don't suppose there are any hotels around here?" she said hopefully. It was getting late. She'd been driving more or less aimlessly all day, trying to make her up mind what to do.

The motel catered to fishermen and hunters. The bed was more like a hammock, but it was clean and cheap, and Clemmie, the woman in the office, told her that the café next door opened at five every morning for breakfast and closed about dark.

Jasmine managed to stay awake long enough to eat a bowl of clam chowder before she fell into bed, too tired to think about tomorrow. A pale sun was shining in through the one small window when she opened her eyes the next morning. She stretched, scratched her left cheek and yawned. And then she scratched again.

Shower. Breakfast. Then maybe spend another day looking around before she went home. As long as she'd come this far, it would be a shame to go back without seeing anything other than a nursing home, a gas station and a cheap motel. She might as well soak up a little atmosphere as long as she'd spent money she couldn't afford to spend just to get here.

Jasmine had never been farther east than Tulsa. There was a different feel to North Carolina. For one thing, it was quieter. Unnaturally quiet, in fact. But that could be because, according to the map, the nearest city was miles away. Or maybe because it was the dead of winter, and here where they had real seasons, things like that made a difference.

By the time she had rinsed off under a trickle of lukewarm water, she felt marginally better. She might even write about it, she thought, idly scratching her face. She hadn't written anything in years, even though she had a perfectly good degree in journalism.

The Further Adventures of Jasmine Clancy. A Thousand Miles From Heartbreak? In Search of Family Ties?

Her stomach growled. How about in search of breakfast?

She was hungry, which was a good sign. Even heartbroken and suffering from acute disappointment, she wasn't bothered by a lack of appetite. In fact, she felt surprisingly good.

That is, she felt good until she looked in the mirror.

"For Pete's sake, what happened to you?" she

whispered, touching her red, swollen face, which instantly began to itch like crazy.

Clemmie was alone in the office, thank goodness. The wife of the owner of the four-unit motel, she did the rooms, helped out in the café, and after one look at Jasmine, she told her to go back to her room.

Twenty minutes later she brought her a breakfast tray of scrambled eggs, sausage and hash browns, with a side order of calamine lotion and a handful of tourist brochures.

"We got these things—mostly nobody ever wants 'em, but since you're not from around here, it might give you something to do. Sort of take your mind off your troubles. If you don't think about it too much, you forget to scratch."

"I can't believe it," Jasmine wailed. "I haven't had poison ivy since I was a child."

"I used to get it real bad, every summer. My mama used to threaten to make me wear boxing gloves to keep me from scratching."

"But it's February!"

"Poison ivy don't die, it just hides out over the winter. Gets you just as bad, though. Now don't scratch, you hear?"

He'd been there for one full week. The first few days he'd nearly gone nuts without his cell phone, his laptop and all the other accoutrements of civilized living he'd grown used to.

Daniel Lyon Lawless, chronological age thirty-seven, physiological age one hundred and seven, rolled over onto his back after the last push-up and stared at a pair of buzzards circling overhead. Maybe they knew something he didn't.

"Not a happy thought," he muttered just to hear the sound of a human voice.

Closing his eyes, he listened to the hollow echo of birds deep inside the boggy forest. Nearby, a frog tuned up. First one, then a dozen. He'd have thought, if he'd thought about frogs at all, they'd be buried in the mud this time of year, but then, what did he know about roughing it in the wilds of the great Dismal Swamp?

Not much. Enough to know that he'd been right to come here, though. In a place like this, away from all distractions, a man could think. If thinking got a little too uncomfortable, he could concentrate on more immediate things, such as keeping the damned bugs from eating him alive. Such as working out until he dropped from exhaustion. Such as wetting a hook in a black-water creek in hope of catching something to relieve a monotonous diet of tinned meat, tinned soup, stale crackers and black coffee.

He had a feeling it wasn't a healthy diet. On the other hand, he'd shed his knee brace three days ago and his back brace the day before that. His cane was no good in this boggy terrain. No good for walking. He carried it anyway, because he felt naked without a weapon, and foolish carrying one here in the back of beyond, where the most dangerous critter he was apt to encounter was a damned mosquito.

He carried a knife, though. It was useful in whacking through vines and opening cans of Vienna sausage. And he walked. He counted it in hours, not miles. He'd done four hours yesterday, on top of six miles rowed back and forth on the nameless creek that bordered his campsite.

Tomorrow he was going to row in one direction until he was exhausted, then he'd go ashore, give his knee a workout and then row himself back to camp. It was a good system. It was working for him. Except for a few minor problems, he was in better shape now than he'd been before the explosion.

He was a hell of a lot more relaxed. Couple of days ago, he'd actually found himself whistling. Another few weeks and he might even find something to smile about.

He wondered what was going on back in Langley. Madden had promised to find out who'd been turned. Who had leaked names, times and places so that two of the best men in the unit had been taken out in one night. Lyon's name would be on that list of expendables. Which was one more reason why he hadn't cared to hang around the hospital like a sitting duck.

A duck on the wing had a far better chance of surviving.

A camcorder. Even a disposable camera. Jasmine would give anything for some way to record what she was seeing. No wonder half of Hollywood had moved to North Carolina, with scenery like this. Moody, spooky, fraught with atmosphere—not to mention the exotic noises and all the different odors. Perfect for a remake of the *Creature from the Black Lagoon*.

At least there were plenty of black lagoons, if mercifully few creatures.

Away from the motel, there was practically no traffic. None at all once she'd left the narrow two-lane highway. Clemmie had told her about the old logging road, and she'd followed it, determined to stay out of public view until her face improved, but wanting to take something back with her after spending the better part of eight hundred dollars on a wild-goose chase.

She'd had sense enough to shove a notepad into her shoulder bag. Clemmie had provided that, too. Her writerly instincts had been stirring all morning. She was even considering doing a travel piece on spec to help pay her expenses.

She might even offer it to one of the two news-papers where she'd briefly worked as a special fea-tures writer before being laid-off, downsized or consolidated, depending on who was offering ex-cuses.

At least it had led to her acting career, which paid at a better rate, only not nearly as regularly.

Fortunately, she was good at rolling with the punches. Going with the flow. Surviving.

The logging road ended at a hill, which turned out to be a mound of rotted sawdust, covered with creep-ing, crawling vines. Something was blooming some-where nearby—something with a sweet, spicy scent.

There was enough high ground so that her feet didn't sink in the mud, so she followed an all but imperceptible trail deeper and deeper into the woods.

Red berries beckoned from the wild tangle of veg-etation. Gorgeous, big fat red berries, like the ones she had picked for her grandmother. Uh-uh. Not again.

She scratched her face, careful not to dig too hard because poison ivy was bad enough without scars. Her face, after all, was her fortune. At five foot ten, her height and her long legs helped, but mostly it was her face. She would like to believe it was her acting ability, because then a few scars might not matter too much, but she was realistic enough to know better.

She had a modest talent and the kind of looks that were just different enough to land her a few parts. Until another kind of look came into fashion, and then she'd do commercials or even catalog work, and maybe some modeling.

Not that modeling appealed to her. The few models she knew were obsessed by diets, cutaneous laser resurfacing, ultrasound liposuctioning. One of them was actually growing her own collagen for when she needed a major overhaul.

Jasmine would much rather settle into a comfortable, low-key life with Eric and their children, and maybe her grandmother living together in a little bungalow somewhere. Fashion was fleeting. Film fame was fleeting. Family was forever.

Oh, yeah? So what happened to all of yours?

Somewhere up ahead she heard a sound that didn't belong in this mystical, moss-hung environment.

A splash. A bump, a yelp...

And then a groan.

TWO

The boat looked out of place in the muted setting. It was painted a muddy shade of royal blue, the paint scuffed in places to reveal a previous coat of turquoise.

Idly, Jasmine scratched her right cheek with her left hand and her left ankle with the toe of her right shoe. When she itched anywhere, she was inclined to itch all over. Power of suggestion.

Either that or mosquito bites.

A canoe would have been good. A dugout canoe would be wonderful, but probably too much to hope for, even in this wilderness. At least it was wooden, not aluminum. It could still belong to a native hunter or trapper or maybe a fisherman with a rich lode of stories to share. Travel pieces with a human interest angle had a far broader appeal. Oklahoma had Will

Rogers. North Carolina had...Daniel Boone? Black-beard?

Well, surely they had somebody interesting. A place like this must have a fascinating history. She'd have to ask Clemmie about it before she checked out tomorrow.

"Hello-oo," she called out tentatively. "Anybody there?"

The sound that greeted her could, she supposed, have come from a hunter or a trapper. As profanity went, it was not particularly original. At least it didn't reek of filth and venom. She didn't mind a few damns and hells when the occasion demanded, but she hated filth and venom.

Whoever it was, he didn't sound as if he were in the mood for company. Carefully, she began to edge away from the creek, or stream or rivulet—whatever it was. According to the map, there was supposed to be a big lake with a name that reminded her of mosquitoes and a river called the Alligator somewhere around here.

What if he was an alligator poacher? She'd read somewhere that hunting alligators was against the law. Jasmine had been called laid-back. She'd never been called stupid.

"I'm leaving now," she sang out, in case he decided to cut the odds of getting caught. "I didn't see anything, so I think I'll just go on back now. Have a nice day."

"Dammit—hold on!"

She held on. It was the kind of voice that commanded obedience. Clutching the straps of her shoulder bag, she held on as if her life depended on it, thinking that in a pinch, she might use it as a weapon.

"I've, um...I'll send somebody if you need help, all right?"

"Need—help!"

He sounded as if he were in pain. Torn between curiosity, concern and a healthy respect for hidden danger—she'd been at an impressionable age when she'd seen *Deliverance*—Jasmine hesitated just a moment too long.

"Can't move. Need—a hand. *Please.*"

That last word was uttered too reluctantly to be anything but sincere. Whoever he was—whatever fix he was in—one thing was clear. He hated like the very devil having to beg for help.

"Sorry, but I'm on the other side of the creek."

That prompted more cursing, and then another, "Please?"

"It looks awfully deep. I can't swim." Even if it was only up to her knees, she wasn't particularly eager to step off the bank into that dark, sluggish stream. She couldn't see a glimmer of bottom. Even if she didn't drown, she might get eaten alive. Maybe not by piranhas, but there might be leeches. She'd seen *African Queen* three times.

"Follow bank—south—forty yards. Fallen tree."

Fallen tree. Uh-huh. "Which way is south?"

She peered through hanging branches, hanging vines and swags of gray-green Spanish moss, trying to catch a glimpse of the man behind the voice. If she was going to take the risk, she'd just as soon know what she was getting involved in.

"Toward sun."

Well, that was easy. As dense as the trees were, there weren't enough leaves to block out the pale, low-riding sun. "Well…all right, I'll try."

Her mind raced ahead as she picked her way along the narrow, winding creek. It could be a heart attack, snakebite—anything. He might even have tripped on one of his own traps and now he was lying there in agony, his lifeblood seeping into the muck while hyenas sniffed at his carcass.

There weren't any hyenas in North America, even she knew that much. That didn't mean there weren't scavengers. Predators.

"Where the devil are you?"

"I'm coming!"

Forty yards. How was she supposed to measure forty yards when every few steps she had to circle around a root or a fallen tree or a tangle of vines—none of them hairy, thank goodness, but some with wicked briars.

There was the tree he'd promised. It had fallen across the creek, blocking two-thirds of its width. Barely enough room to squeak past in a boat, if he'd come from this direction.

And he must have come from this direction, because he'd known about the tree.

Scratching her cheek—not actually scratching, but pressing into the itch with her fingernails—Jasmine surveyed the situation. If she could keep her balance, keep from falling in, she might be able to walk out far enough to jump the rest of the way. That's if she didn't lose her nerve first.

She lost her nerve, but it was too late. Teetering on the lower edge of the huge trunk, she faced two choices. Turn around on the mossy rounded slope and go back...or jump.

She jumped.

"Ow! Oh, shoot!"

"What happened?" His voice held an edge that could have come from pain, or it could have come from anger. She'd like to think it came from pain.

Well, that didn't sound very nice, either. She certainly didn't wish the man any more pain. All the same, an angry man—an angry strange man, all alone here in the wilds of the jungle...

Not jungle—swamp. There was a subtle difference, although she wasn't certain just what it was.

No lions or tigers, only alligators and poisonous snakes?

Oh, God, why didn't I stay home? Being a bridesmaid couldn't be much worse than this.

At least this place was on the map. It had a name.

Dismal. Oh, great. She slapped at a mosquito and swore a mild oath. This probably wasn't the dumbest thing she'd ever done, but it was right up there near the top of the list.

"What happened?" he called again.

"Nothing happened! I landed on my knees in the mud," she yelled back.

She was filthy. No more scratching, at least not until she'd scrubbed her fingernails with soap and water. Unless she used a stick. A twig. Natural things were naturally sanitary, weren't they? Hadn't she read that somewhere?

Sure they were. Like natural poison ivy.

Lyon had plenty of time for second thoughts while he lay there waiting for deliverance, his face set in a grimace of pain. He'd tried ignoring the agonizing spasms in his back. He'd tried forcing himself to relax, muscle by muscle. He'd tried mind over matter, but pain was pain, and his mind wasn't up to the task.

Here she came. It would have to be a female. With his luck, she'd be one of those environmentalists, ready to land on him with both feet for disturbing the pristine wilderness with his beer bottle and his Vienna sausage can and his crass human intrusion.

He could have told her the possums would eat the grease. The can would eventually rust away. They did still make 'em out of tin, didn't they? As for the bottle, he'd take the damned thing with him if she could just help him get on his feet and back in his boat. Eventually, he'd drift back to the campsite.

Eventually. Like maybe, in a couple of weeks.

Either she was wearing snowshoes or she was leading a troop of cub scouts. He heard her thrashing through the underbrush long before she came into sight.

Long. That was his first thought. That she was long all over, especially her legs, which were pink and white and muddy. That she was wearing a fright wig the color of raw venison that stood out around her face like a halo, only he'd never seen a halo in that shade of red, nor one decorated with leaves, cypress needles and twigs.

She smiled. It was a surprisingly sweet smile in what would have been a pretty face except that there was something wrong with it. He wanted to tell her she shouldn't go around smiling at strange men that way. For all she knew, he could be dangerous, only she could probably tell by the way he was lying here flat on his back sweating bullets that he was no threat to anyone.

"Did you fall?" She had a nice voice when she wasn't yelling; low, husky—no discernible accent. Even half dead, his brain automatically noted and filed away such details.

"Not recently." At her look of puzzlement, he added, "Bad back. Took off brace, rowed too far in one stretch." He sort of grunted the words, trying to keep from breathing too deeply because every breath he took was sheer agony.

She sat on her haunches beside him, her knees projecting over his chest. God, didn't the woman have a grain of sense under that fright wig?

A man would have to be dead not to react to all that satiny white skin, even when it was daubed with mud and laced with red scratches.

He drew a cautious breath, inhaling the scent of perfume, calamine and feminine sweat.

"Never wear perfume in a swamp," he grunted.

"I know. I only wore it to, um—boost my morale, but it draws mosquitoes. Is it sort of like a Charly horse?"

"Your perfume?"

"Your back."

He kept staring at her. Jasmine was used to being stared at; she was a minor celebrity, after all. A very, very minor one.

Somehow, she didn't think that was the reason he was staring at her. What did she expect her to do? She was no medical missionary. She'd never even been a Girl Scout. They'd moved around too much.

"Yeah, sort of," he said through clenched teeth.

He had nice teeth. White, even, but not quite perfect. They showed to an advantage in a face that was covered in several days' growth of beard.

He closed his eyes. Without the distraction of a pair of intense periwinkle blue eyes, he looked tired and miserable. Logic told her she had no business being there. Instinct told her that he was harmless and that he desperately needed her help.

Jasmine always trusted her instincts. Every time she went against them—as in the case of Eric—she lived to regret it.

"So...what can I do to help you? Go for help?"

"No!"

He winced, as if speaking sharply hurt him. If she didn't know better, she might even have thought he was afraid of something.

Of course, she didn't know better. For all she knew, he was a criminal on the run. Might even have been injured in a shoot-out, only she didn't see any sign of blood.

"Are you a criminal?" she asked. Might as well get everything out in the open. He didn't appear to be armed, and she was pretty sure she could outrun him, if push came to shove.

"No way," he gasped. "Retired...cop."

"You're too young to be retired, and how do I know you're a cop?"

"Disability," Lyon said, not without a glimmer of humor. Damn, she was persistent. If he'd had to be rescued by a female, why couldn't she have been a physical therapist?

"Then you really are a policeman?"

He nodded, which was a mistake, the neckbone be-

ing connected to the backbone, et cetera, et cetera. He
wasn't a cop and he wasn't retired, but it was close
enough to the truth.

Close enough for government work, as the old saying went.

"Well. I don't suppose you can walk, but if we can
get you in the boat maybe I can take you back to the
motel and have someone send for a doctor. It's right
on the water. The motel, I mean. It might even be on
the main river, I'm not sure, but if it is, this stream
should get us there sooner or later. All we have to do
is follow—"

"No way."

"No way, what? Everything east of the Mississippi
flows into the ocean by way of streams and rivers. If
we—"

"No, I mean—ah, hell, it hurts!" Lyon closed his
eyes and willed himself to let go—not to tense up.
"Get me back to my campsite and we'll call it even."

"I don't see anything even about that. I do all the
work and you—"

"And I do all the bitching and groaning. Sorry
about that. I'll pay you for your time."

"I don't want your money." She had dark eyes—
brown with a hint of maroon, like her hair. They were
shooting off sparks.

"Take off, then. Sooner or later someone else will
come by." They both knew that was a crock. They
were so deep into uncharted territory it was a wonder
the buzzards could even find them. "How'd you get
here? The road doesn't come anywhere near here."

"I followed an old logging road and then just kept
on walking."

"Why?"

"Why not?"

"Lady, that's no answer, but if it's all right with you, I'd just as soon skip the dialogue and head on back to camp. You wouldn't believe how dark it can get this far from the nearest streetlight."

Jasmine was no judge of distance. There was a security light outside the motel, but that would be miles away. Miles and miles and miles. The trouble with long legs was that they covered so much territory, even at a leisurely pace. "If I can get you into your boat, can you do the rest by yourself?"

He gave her that "Duh" look.

"Okay, so maybe I'll paddle you as far as your camp—and even help you get out, but then I'll have to get back to the motel. I'm catching a plane to L.A. tomorrow."

She was catching a plane nowhere, no time soon. That much quickly became obvious. By the time she managed to get him into the boat, they were both practically in tears. He from pain; she from sheer exasperation.

Not to mention the fact that he was about a hundred eighty pounds of solid muscle and bone, and fighting her all the way. Or if not her, fighting the pain.

She'd have sympathized more if he hadn't cursed under his breath every step of the way. "Relax," she snapped.

"Lady, if I could relax, I wouldn't be here."

"Fine. Then don't relax. If I had a brain, I wouldn't be here, either."

The fighting didn't stop at the edge of the water. "It's not a paddle, it's a damned oar!"

"I know what it is, and stop cursing."

"Then stop jiggling around and sit down."

She sat. On the back seat, because he was sprawled out across the front seat, taking up most of the middle space. He was sweating. It wasn't really cold, even though it was February, but it wasn't warm, either. Especially not now that the sun was almost out of sight.

Jasmine wished, not for the first time, that she'd worn jeans instead of her white shorts. And a jacket instead of a long-sleeve yellow denim shirt. She was a summer person. She didn't own clothes suitable for a North Carolina winter.

"Don't you even know how to row a boat?"

"Of course I know how to row a boat." She'd seen it done plenty of times in the movies.

"You don't row from the stern thwart, you row from amidship."

"I know that."

"Then move!"

"You're there. Amidship, I mean." He was propped up against a seat cushion on the whatsis up front, but his legs stretched out so that his feet were under the middle seat.

"Straddle my damned feet!"

She'd rather straddle his damned neck. With her bare hands.

But she moved, rocking the boat, causing him to gasp so that she was thoroughly ashamed of herself. The man was injured. She didn't really want to hurt him any worse than he was already hurting, but if anyone deserved a bit of pain, he probably did.

Once settled on the edge of the wooden seat, she eyed him cautiously and reached for the oars. There were no oarlocks, only wooden notches that had been wallowed out until they were all but useless.

The oars stretched almost all the way across the creek. Cypress knees reached out from both sides. Lyon could have told her she'd need to shove from the stern until they cleared the fallen gum. Once past that point, the creek widened out.

He didn't tell her because the last thing he needed was a clumsy, clueless beanpole dancing around in the stern of his boat. They'd both end up overboard, and he'd sink like a stone.

She muttered enough so that he pinned down her accent. Bible Belt with a faint patina of West Coast, polished by a few diction lessons. He wondered what the devil she was doing here, and then he quit wondering about anything except whether or not he would survive the night.

If he could've gotten his hands on all those muscle relaxants he'd quit taking cold turkey, he'd have downed the lot. And then, if he was still capable of unscrewing a cap, he'd have started in on the painkillers.

She shipped the oars as they approached the fallen gum tree. One of them swiveled around and struck him in the shoulder. The other one rolled across his shin.

"Oops. Sorry," she said. "It's getting dark. How far is this camp place of yours?"

"About six and three-quarters miles."

Her mouth fell open. She had a nice mouth, well curved, full lower lip, but not too full. The swelling on her right cheek and eye was probably poison ivy. Even with most of his attention taken up by his own situation, he'd noticed her trying not to scratch. She'd reach up, hesitate, frown at her grimy nails and sigh. He'd have scratched it for her if his back had permitted him to reach out.

"I can't go that far, I have to get back to the motel."

"Fine. Pull over to the bank and get out."

"What about you?"

"What about me? I won't starve, if that's what you're worried about. I had half a can of Vienna sausage for lunch."

"How will you get home?"

"Not your problem."

"It is so my problem! I can't see my way back to the motel in the dark. I'll take you to your camp and you can lend me a flashlight and point me in the direction of the road, and…"

She gaped at him, her mahogany-colored eyes growing round. Even the one that was swollen half shut. "Did you say six and three-quarter *miles?*" she whispered.

The boat scraped against a cypress knee, and without even looking, she reached out, grabbed the thing and shoved off. Her survival skills were on a par with her rowing ability.

"Like I said, pull over to the bank and get out. Follow the creek to where you found me and then retrace your steps back to wherever you came from." If he'd known there was a motel within walking distance, he might have gone even deeper into the swamp.

Company, he didn't need.

Jasmine was having trouble making out his features. He was facing away from the rapidly fading light. His shoulders looked enormous in the baggy gray sweatshirt. She had a feeling they would look even more impressive without it. A surly man with shoulders the size of a refrigerator she didn't need.

With a heavy sigh, she retrieved the oars now that the creek had widened out. One of them scraped his hip. He caught his breath, she apologized, and told herself it would make a wonderful travel piece. Lost in the wilderness, surrounded by silence, Spanish moss, cypress knees and a perfectly splendid sunset that was reflected, now that she'd come around a bend, on the water.

So far she'd seen no signs of any predators, but she had seen a huge, graceful bird she recognized as a heron type. It lifted from the bank just as they'd rounded the bend and flapped right overhead. If she'd been standing, she could have reached out and touched it.

If she'd been standing, she would have probably fallen overboard. Heaven help her if that happened, because she couldn't swim a stroke and whatsisname wouldn't be able to pull her out.

"What is your name, anyway?" She slapped at a mosquito and winced when it set off her itching again.

He hesitated just long enough for her to wonder why he hesitated at all. "Lyon," he said.

"Oh, right. As long as it's not alligator."

"What's yours?"

She didn't hesitate. She, at least, had nothing to hide. "Jasmine. Jasmine Clancy," she said, just in case he was wondering where he might have seen her before.

"Great. That takes care of the flora and fauna."

"Ha-ha, very funny. How far is it now?"

"At a guess, I'd say about five and a half miles."

She groaned. She'd been rowing steadily ever since the creek widened. Thanks to his constant carping, she was beginning to get the hang of it, but her hands would never be the same. "I don't suppose you have a pair of gloves, do you?"

"I'm sorry." Actually, Lyon thought, she wasn't all that bad. Her form was lousy, but what she lacked in physical strength, she made up for in determination. He should have thought about her hands, though. If he could have got to his knife, she could have hacked off his sleeves and pulled them over her hands like a mitt.

Jasmine felt tears sting her eyes. She hated pain, she really did. She hated itching, hated mosquitoes, hated noxious vines that hated her right back, but most of all, she hated being here in the middle of the wilderness, not knowing where she was or how she was ever going to get back.

She was a coward. She'd always been a coward. After her father left, she and her mother never stayed in the same place more than a year or two. She used to wake up in the middle of the night terrified that she would come home from school and find her mother gone, too, and strangers living in her house.

She leaned forward—from the hips, the way he'd told her—and bumped the oars against the wallowed-out wooden oarlocks. Dammit, she would get him there if it killed her! She refused to be put out in the middle of this damned swamp in the dead of night, without so much as a flashlight.

"Take a break."

"It won't help."

"Do it. I've got a handkerchief. Dig it out of my hip pocket, rip it in two pieces and wrap it around your palms."

She really didn't want to break her rhythm. And she had one, she really did. He had a lousy disposition. He'd fussed at her constantly, but he'd taught her the rudiments of rowing a boat.

Taught her enough to know that if she never set foot in one of the damned things again, it would be too soon.

"Do it, Jasmine. I don't want you bleeding all over me."

"Why, because you're afraid the scent of fresh blood might attract alligators?" She lost her rhythm. A blade caught the water and jerked at her arm, and she uttered a five-letter word. Tears trickled down her cheeks, making her rash itch all the more.

"At least when I hit the headlines—Actress Lost in Damned Dismal Swamp, Feared Dead—my grandmother won't recognize my name."

Three

The sky was beginning to grow pale when Lyon opened his eyes. Being careful not to move, he drew a shallow, experimental breath. He still hurt. Hurt like hell, in fact, and where he didn't hurt, he ached. The difference was subtle, but it was there.

He toyed with it as his senses came quickly alive. Mental exercises served a purpose when physical exercise was out of the question.

Like now. A fourteen-foot skiff was no place to spend a night. Especially not with a broken back and a knee that was still none too reliable.

Especially not an open skiff. In February. The warm spell was over. The temperature must've dropped into the forties last night.

They'd stopped for a rest. Her hands had been hurting. He'd been hurting all over. He'd known there was no hope of reaching camp before dark, and rather than risk taking a wrong turn, he'd let her sleep. And then he'd fallen asleep himself. Not a smart thing to do, but then, his options weren't exactly limitless.

"Ah, hell," he muttered, gazing bleary-eyed at the woman still huddled in the stern of the boat. She'd turned up the collar of her shirt, rolled down her sleeves and done her best to cover those long, naked legs with a few rumpled tissues and the flap of her shoulder bag.

"Wake up," he rasped.

She groaned and tried to draw her knees up to her chin. Her no-longer-white shorts weren't particularly skimpy. They'd been designed to come halfway down her thighs, but when a woman had legs as long as hers, there was still a lot of flesh left exposed to the elements.

Not to mention exposed to the eyes.

"Jasmine, look alive. We've got to get some heat going."

"Turnip therm'stat."

"Right. You do it—you're the closest."

She opened one eye. The other one was swollen shut. Shivering, she mumbled something that sounded like "Where Nell ama?"

"By my reckoning, you're approximately five miles north of Billy's Landing, about half a mile west of Two Buzzard Ditch, and a mile or so east of Graceland."

"Oh."

She scratched her cheek and then her ankle, and smiled. There was something dangerously disarming about a woman who woke up shivering, scratching, blinking one eye and still managed to smile.

She yawned, rearranging splotched remnants of calamine lotion. "Graceland? I thought that was in Tennessee." Her voice was early-morning soft. Husky. In another woman, under other circumstances, he might have taken it as an invitation.

With Jasmine he took it as merely easy on the ears.

"Bad joke. Think you can do a few warm-ups without falling overboard? We need to get your blood circulating."

"Too late. 'S frozen like a raspberry snow cone."

He yawned, too. And then, unexpectedly, he grinned. Couldn't recall the last time he'd smiled, especially before breakfast, but she seemed to have that effect on him.

Lyon had come here to be alone. If he had to have company, he'd have preferred a chiropractor or a physical therapist. Instead, he got Jasmine Clancy with her poison ivy and her blistered hands and her world-class legs. He wasn't sure just what breed of woman she was, but she didn't belong here. One way or another, he probably ought to get rid of her.

"How're you doing? Back still broken?" she asked in a voice that reminded him of late nights, rumpled beds and soft women.

"It's better." It was worse. A hell of a lot worse, but there was no point in giving her all the bad news at once. "Are you hungry?"

"Starved. I don't suppose this yacht of yours runs to a galley?"

"Chef's night out. If you can manage to get your

hand into my left side pocket, you might find half a chocolate bar. It'll be messy, I'm afraid."

"I'll take it."

It wasn't quite as simple as it sounded. She eased herself up to a kneeling position, but in doing so, she was forced to straddle his legs. The boat rocked. She grabbed the sides, winced at the pain and waited for things to calm down again.

Lyon waited for her to recover her balance, grab the thing out of his pocket and get the hell off his lap. He would have dug it out himself if he hadn't been afraid to move anything connected to his back. Which included his arms.

Fine pair they were. He shifted slightly to give her access. Cargo pants had plenty of storage room. He didn't particularly want her exploring it all.

Cautiously, she dragged one knee alongside his legs and leaned forward to slide one hand into his left side pocket. Her hair tickled his face. It was wilder than ever—probably hadn't seen a comb in days—and it smelled faintly of...lilac?

Oh, hell, if there was one thing he didn't need it was a woman who smelled of lilacs. "Come on, come on, we don't have all day," he growled.

He was discovering—rediscovering, at least—things about himself that he'd just as soon have left safely buried for another few years.

Such as the fact that the male of the species was about ten parts brain to ninety parts testosterone. If there was one thing he didn't need screwing up his ten percent at the moment, it was that other ninety percent.

Her fingers fumbled against his groin. He could

kick himself for not wearing a shirt with pockets. He could kick himself for not eating the whole damned thing instead of saving half for the trip back to the campsite in case he ran out of energy.

She dug out a knife, a pocket calculator and a shapeless lump that was half a chocolate bar that had melted and stuck to the wrapper. "Don't you want any? One bite, that's all I need. Just enough to wake me up. Chocolate has caffeine, doesn't it?"

"Nah, I don't want any. You eat it all, you're the one who's going to have to get us out of here."

So then he had to watch while she unwrapped the thing and licked it off the paper. Nearby, a small flock of fish ducks dived for breakfast. A great blue squawked a protest and lifted from the banks, long legs dangling gracefully.

He scowled at the birds and then he scowled at her long, graceful, mud-stained, briar-scratched legs. And then he scowled some more just on general principle. "We'd better get going. If you want to go ashore for a minute, there's a place just downstream from here where the bank's pretty clear."

"I'm thirsty. I don't suppose you have anything to drink, do you?"

"Warm beer?"

She shuddered. "I'll wait for coffee, thanks. You will offer me a cup of coffee before I head back to the motel, won't you?"

He shrugged, which was a painful mistake, but it was all the answer she was going to get. He'd offer her coffee, all right, but she wouldn't be going back. Not anytime soon.

As dainty as if it were a perfumed finger bowl, she

dipped her hands over the sides, swished them around, then wet a tissue and daubed at her face.

Pity. He'd been admiring the rim of chocolate around her mouth. Shifting painfully into the most comfortable position he could achieve for the long trip ahead, he said, "You missed the spot beside your nose. No—left side. Got it."

And then he had to wait while she took a brush from her purse and set to work on her hair. "I won't be much longer," she said when she caught him staring at her. "It's just that I can think better once I've washed and brushed. I'd give anything if I had my toothbrush."

Closing his eyes, Lyon braced himself to endure the next few hours.

"This is it?" Jasmine shipped the oars. He'd used the phrase earlier and she liked the sound of it. It sounded...brisk. Decisive. If there was one thing she could use about now, it was a shot of brisk decisiveness.

He appeared to be waiting for further comment. When none was forthcoming, he began the painful, awkward business of getting to his feet. She offered to help.

"Just stand back, okay? No, don't touch me!"

She wasn't about to touch him.

Well, yes...maybe she had reached out to him, but that was purely instinctive. It would take someone really heartless to stand by and watch a man suffer the way Lion—Lion?—the way he was suffering. "Watch out for the wet place on the floor," she cautioned.

"Deck."

"I knew that."

The look he sent her would have blistered paint. "Hold the boat steady when I start to swing my left leg over the side, will you?"

She grabbed the sides. Her hands hurt like the very devil, but she grabbed and held on until something in the way he was looking at her tipped her off that this wasn't what he'd had in mind.

Crouched over, one hand on his back, the other gripping the scarred wooden trim that ran all the way around the edge of the boat, he glared at her over his shoulder.

Jasmine glared right back. "I'm doing the best I can. If you don't like it, hire someone else."

Under the heavy growth of beard, his face was roughly the color of wet plaster. He was sweating. The temperature had to be somewhere around zero minus ten. Personally, Jasmine had never been colder in her entire life than she'd been last night, and he was sweating.

"Pick up one of the oars," he said through clenched teeth.

She picked it up. He obviously read her mind, because he said, "If you're going to knock me in the head, wait until I'm on shore, will you? You don't want to show up at your motel with a dead man on board. Too much explaining to do."

She took a deep breath, puffed out her cheeks, which made her face start itching all over again, and said with deceptive mildness, "All right, I'm holding onto the oar. I'm pretty sure this one won't try to get away, but what about the other one?"

Ignoring her sarcasm, he told her what to do. "Jab it in the mud as far up on the bank as you can reach and hang on. If you feel the boat start to move away, pull it in again."

"Why not use an anchor?"

He closed his eyes. His lips were moving. *One, two, three, four...* "Because I don't have a damned anchor, all right?"

"Doesn't the Coast Guard require stuff like that in all boats?"

"Just jam the damned oar into the mud and hold on long enough for me to get out, will you? Then you can go find the nearest Coast Guard station and turn me in!"

Well. It wasn't her fault he didn't have all the required equipment. Selecting a place on the bank that looked relatively root-free and damp, she clutched the oar and lunged. The boat rocked. Lyon groaned. And then he swore.

"If you're going to jump out, hurry up. I can't hold us here all day." She closed her eyes against the fire in her palms. Both hands hurt all the way up to her armpits. She felt the boat lurch and opened her eyes just as the man landed on the shore. Mostly on shore. Parts of him hung over the bank, one foot touching the water.

"If this is the Alligator River, you're asking for trouble." And if her voice sounded funny, it was because she was trying not to cry. Itching was bad enough. Freezing was even worse. The way her hands hurt was worst of all, because it meant they were totally raw, and as dirty as she was, she'd get infected and everybody knew there were germs these days that thumbed their noses at antibiotics. Flesh eating germs.

Or was it viruses? Organisms?

Whatever.

"What the hell are you waiting for?" growled the man in the mud. He was lying belly down, making no effort to get up, but of course, he couldn't without excruciating pain.

If she wanted to get away, this was her chance. All she had to do was walk off and leave him. He could hardly come after her.

On the other hand, she could hardly leave him here in this condition. It wouldn't be kind.

Besides, there was no sign of a road. No sign of anything except for a small clearing, a tiny fire pit, a metal trunk of some sort and a scrap of camouflage-colored tent hardly big enough for a small Boy Scout.

She'd seen better outfitted bag ladies, and said so, which elicited another groan from the shore.

"If you're going to go, then shove off. Go back the way you came, leave the boat on the bank. Chances are it'll still be there when I get around to collecting it."

"Oh, sure, just paddle off and leave you sprawled out for the hyenas and buzzards to finish off, right?"

"Don't forget the alligators."

"And the mosquitoes." Irritably, she waved off a swarm of the pesky things. She hated the whining sound they made almost as much as she hated the itchy welts they raised on her unprotected skin. Which was just about all of it.

Taking the piece of rope he called a painter, that was tied to a rusty eye in the front of the boat, she gripped it tightly between her thumb and fingers and jumped for the shore. This time she landed on her feet.

"If you're waiting for applause, forget it," he said after half a minute or so. "How about helping me to my feet."

"Why not just lie around for a while? You probably need the rest."

"What I need is to use the can, if you'll pardon my indelicacy."

She blushed. She, who had heard more and seen more of life before she was fifteen years old than some women did in a lifetime. She, an experienced woman of the world who'd had one-and-a-half lovers, blushed at the mention of a bathroom.

Thank goodness, what with the dirt and poison ivy and all, it couldn't possibly show. She'd have been laughed right out of L.A.

Getting the Lion into an upright position again was almost as bad as getting him into the boat had been, the only difference being that neither of them was likely to fall overboard and drown.

"Can you swim?" she asked. She was leaning against a tree, both hands cupped in front of her, examining them for signs of imminent infection.

Lyon was making his cautious way toward the swag of vines that separated the slit trench he'd dug just yesterday from the rest of his campsite. "Yeah. Why?"

He didn't like questions, even dumb questions from a gorgeous, lopsided, long-legged dodo bird.

"I dunno, I just thought I'd ask."

"Well, don't. I told you, if you want to clear out,

feel free. Now that I'm back on familiar territory, I'll
be fine."

"Is that where the bathroom is?" She nodded toward the tangle of vines and underbrush. "I need to
freshen up when you're done."

Freshen up. Sure. "I'll put out a clean towel."

She blushed again, and this time he caught it.
Caught it and grinned, in spite of the fact that he was
sweaty, buggy, his bladder was fit to burst and with
every breath he took he felt as if a dozen dull knives
were excavating his spinal column.

"No point in waiting. Walk five yards in any direction and you're out of sight. There's paper in the
locker, soap and a towel if you need it. You'll have
to use the creek, though. City water doesn't come out
this far."

She was already picking her way carefully across
the clearing, still holding her hands as if they hurt
like the very devil. They probably did. "Hey, wash
your hands good with soap, and I'll fix 'em up for
you, okay?"

Evidently, she took him at his word. Five minutes
later, he heard a splash, a gasp and then a yelp. Soap
and water on raw flesh was no picnic.

But then, what was?

And that reminded him that neither of them had
eaten since yesterday, other than half a melted bar of
chocolate. He washed his hands, using the rainwater
he'd collected in a hollow stump, and surveyed his
supplies, moving slowly, stiffly, smothering the occasional curse.

Brunch was Vienna sausage, cold, canned chili and
warm beer. "Sorry I don't have any sodas. Never

touch the stuff. Too many chemicals.''

Jasmine wrinkled her nose, touched her cheek gingerly with a bandaged hand, and jiggled the gauze against the itch. ''This is fine. I always intended to cultivate a taste for beer.''

''The creek water's probably okay, but I don't believe in taking chances.''

She nodded. Sitting cross-legged on a log, she forked out another sausage and bit it in two. A zillion calories and all of them fat, but don't drink the water. Some people were weird.

''So. You never did say what you were doing here in the jungle all by yourself,'' she ventured after a while.

''No, I never did, did I? How's your face? Still itching?''

''Not until you reminded me.''

''Want coffee for dessert?''

''Made from warm beer?''

''I don't waste valuable beer. I only brought in a dozen six-packs.''

''Why?''

''Why what?'' They'd played this game before. The girl asking questions, trying to slip in under his guard and pry loose a few answers. He could have told her, but didn't, that he'd been interrogated by experts.

''Why'd you bring in so much beer?''

''Because I like beer.''

She sighed. He liked to watch her sigh. She put more feeling into a single sigh than most women did a crying fit and two tantrums. He was inclined to believe she was on the level, not that it mattered. Once he got rid of her he'd move to a different location. He was good at covering his tracks.

While she was still here—and that would be longer than either one of them wanted—she couldn't contact anyone. Until and unless he caught her flashing mirrors or launching notes in a bottle, he'd keep her.

Slipping off the log onto the leaf-covered ground, she said, "Well," and patted her flat belly, white gauze mitts contrasting against her once-white shorts. "Thanks for the meal and the first aid. I'd better take a pass on the coffee and get started back if I want to get there before dark."

Lyon studied her without appearing to. It was a minor talent he'd honed to a fine art. God, she was a mess. That hair—the poison ivy. All the mud and the scratches. He'd like nothing better than to lay her down in a bed of leaves and spend a few hours practicing another art.

Funny, the way she affected him. She wasn't at all his type. He liked his women short, busty, blond and temporary.

Jasmine Clancy was none of the above. And even if she happened to be willing, he sure as hell wasn't able. He could barely move. Bed-sport was totally out of the question.

Pity, though. There was something about her that could easily light his fuse under other circumstances. He didn't understand it. Anything he didn't understand became a challenge.

"Do I need to cross the creek to reach the road?"

"Huh?" He'd been thinking about something else. About fuses, and how uncomfortable a smoldering one could be when letting it burn to the logical end was out of the question.

"The road. I was just saying, I hope it's on this side of the creek or river or whatever, because I don't think I can row another stroke." She held up both hands. They'd been in bad shape. It amazed him that she hadn't complained, either about her hands or about sleeping uncovered in an open boat in February, even if it was the mildest February in years.

If he'd been any sort of a gentleman he'd have stripped off his sweatshirt and covered her up. Not that he could've moved to do it. Not that he'd even thought about it. Too many other things on his mind.

Anyway, he'd never pretended to be a gentleman.

Still, he mused, it might have been interesting to see how warm he could keep her.

His voice softened to a gravelly rasp, which was about as close to apologetic as it got. "Look, why not stick around awhile. I mean, I know you have a plane to catch, but you've already missed it by now, so why not relax and enjoy a wilderness experience? Once you're back in L.A. you can tell all your friends how you survived being lost in the Great Eastern Dismal Swamp all alone."

"Hardly alone."

"Makes a better story that way."

"Hmm." She looked thoughtful. He wondered what she'd look like without the poison ivy. He wondered what she was really doing here. First chance he got he intended to go through her purse. A guy in his position couldn't afford too many scruples.

"But I'm not lost, am I?"

She sounded so worried he nearly relented and told

her she could go if she could find her way out. He
didn't really need her. Hell, she needed him more
than he needed her.

All the same, going back was not an option. Not
just yet. "No, you're not lost. I know exactly where
we are."

It took half the afternoon for full realization to sink
in. Lyon didn't push it. It was better if she figured it
out all by herself. Then she couldn't blame him.

"You knew I couldn't row myself back with my
hands like this, didn't you?" she accused.

Without thinking, he shrugged and then winced as
the knives attacked again. "Depends on your pain
threshold."

"Why does it hurt worse now than it did before
you spread that yucky stuff on me and bandaged me
up?"

He started to shrug again and caught himself just
in time. "Maybe because you're starting to heal?
Healing usually hurts."

"Is that what's wrong with you? You're healing?"

"I'd damned well better be." He was wearing his
back brace again. She'd had to help him get the thing
on. Help him get his shirt off, and then reach around
him with both arms and help him fasten the velcro
straps. He'd been in worse shape when they'd finished
than when they'd started, and not just his back.

"But if I took your boat, how would you get it
back? And don't tell me to leave it where I found it,
because I'm not sure I can even locate the place again,
and even if I do, you're in no condition to walk that
far."

"So you noticed that, did you?"

"Don't look at me like that, like I'm stupid. I'm not. Only, you knew exactly what you were doing, bringing me here, didn't you? You didn't even care if I was inconvenienced." She glared at him. She had a very effective glare. Funny, he'd never before noticed how many different shades of brown eyes came in. As a rule he was a noticing man. In his line of work, lives could depend on it.

"Yes, well—I guess I don't have to go back right away. My reservations are not until the end of the week, but that doesn't mean I intend to hang around here any longer than I have to. I don't even have a toothbrush, for goodness sake. Everything I own is back at the motel."

He nodded. "Duly noted."

"So, how far's the road from here?"

"I haven't a clue."

Her eyes accused him of lying.

"I haven't looked for a road. As far as I know, the nearest trail of any kind is about two, maybe three miles away." He'd purposefully looked for a place with a single access. No place was foolproof, but this one was close. He'd been here nearly two weeks, and flower girl was the first person he'd seen. Evidently, there wasn't a whole lot of traffic in the middle of the swamp this time of year. Too late for hunting—too early for fishing. The site he'd selected was located between a couple of wildlife preserves. Any tourists in the area would go there, not here. He was banking on it.

"Then what are you doing here? Are you sure you're not hiding out?"

"What if I told you I'm a celebrity hiding out from the paparazzi?"

"I wouldn't believe you. Besides, if you were a celebrity, I'd recognize you, and I don't."

"Okay, how about I'm a millionaire hiding out from the IRS?"

"Any self-respecting millionaire would have better camping gear. You don't even have a decent tent."

"This region's known for the hunting and fishing."

"So where's your gun and fishing pole?"

Lyon was amused. It had been a long time since he'd been amused. He could've shown her both items, but she might tumble to the fact that neither the Glock nor the Sig-Sauer 9mm would pass as hunting equipment. Instead, he said, "Okay, my turn. What's a woman like you doing in a place like this?"

"You brought me here?"

"Uh-uh. You brought *me* here, remember?"

By that time they were both grinning. It felt good. Lyon couldn't remember the last time he'd flashed his pearlies twice in as many hours.

"About that coffee," he reminded her. "If you'll dip us a potful of water, I'll see what I can do about getting a fire going."

"Let me. I don't want you to strain your back. One way or another I plan to leave first thing tomorrow, and I'd feel bad about leaving you here hurting."

Four

"**S**top!"

Jasmine teetered on the brink, arms flapping wildly.

"Dammit, don't do that!" he yelled.

"Don't do what?" Exasperation sharpened her husky voice.

"Don't even think about stealing my boat. You'd never make it back to civilization."

"What's the matter, are you afraid I'll get lost and then you'd have me on your conscience?" Planting her bandaged hands on her hips, she gave him her best shot at scathing contempt. She'd never done scathing contempt very well. It wasn't in her repertoire, but she was working on it.

"Yes, you'd get lost, and no, I wouldn't have you on my conscience." He did scathing contempt exceedingly well. Academy award performance. "I don't have a conscience."

She snorted. "Everyone has a conscience. Every decent, normal person."

"Who said anything about being decent?"

Lyon watched her eyes widen. The swelling was coming down on the side of her face. Her eyes almost matched now. It was an improvement.

He didn't need any improvements. Not in her appearance, at any rate. She was enough of a distraction as it was. Wearing one of his T-shirts, a leather windbreaker and a pair of his jeans bundled around her waist, with six inches of elegant ankle hanging out the south end, she was driving him crazy.

"Help me get into this damned knee brace again, will you?"

She looked as if she might consider it. Then again, she might not.

"Please?" he added grudgingly. Even to his own ears, it sounded more like two big feet landing in a bed of gravel. Neither one of them was ever apt to center a stage at the Metropolitan Opera. He didn't know what her excuse was; his was having his larynx damned near shattered by a flying foot back in his training days.

"Stick out your leg then."

"Lady, if I could stick out my leg, I wouldn't need you." He was sitting on a stump, his back stiff as a poker, trying to figure out how he could get up without moving a muscle.

She waited a full minute, and then she stalked over to him like a stiff-legged dog in a yard full of cats. "I wasn't going to steal your old boat."

"I know you weren't." Gradually, clasping his

thigh, he eased his knee into position while she knelt in front of him and rolled up his pants leg.

She frowned. She had a nice frown. Puckers between her eyebrows, pursed lips. Yeah, she had a nice frown.

Holding the black elastic contraption in one hand, she reached under his knee, which brought her head close enough so that her hair brushed his skin. He stiffened, caught his breath as his back protested, and swore silently.

He'd almost rather be back in the hospital. At least there he hadn't felt like such a crock. Hospitals were full of crocks. And none of the nurses had tickled his knee with their hair at a time when he was in no condition to do anything about it.

"Why'd you accuse me of it, then?"

"Accuse you of what?"

"Stealing your boat."

For once in his life, he'd spoken without thinking. It wasn't the boat he'd been worried about, it was the woman. He'd been afraid she might slip on the muddy bank and hurt herself.

Yeah, sure you were. You were afraid she might leave you, weren't you? "Actually, I was afraid you were going to jump in the creek and try to swim back."

"I would've changed into my own clothes first. I wouldn't have stolen yours."

"I can't tell you how relieved I am," he snarled, and then damn near bit his tongue off when her fingers brushed over the sensitive place behind his knee.

"Besides, I can't swim."

"Good." With half his supply of sterile gauze

wrapped around her palms, she was taking forever. He'd like to tell her to bug off, and do the job himself, but there was no way he could manage without either bringing his knee up within reach of his hands or bending his back. At the moment, neither option was viable.

Jaw clenched, he stared down at the top of her head. Sunlight filtered through the bare gum branches, spinning rainbows of color around every wild, curly strand of her hair. He concentrated on the colors instead of on the warm moisture of her breath against his naked thigh.

"There's nothing good about it," she grumbled. "All children should be taught to swim at an early age. How'd you get these scars, anyway?"

"Falling off the back of an elephant. Why weren't you?" He was on to her tricks now. She'd muddle along at a moderate speed just long enough to throw him off guard, and then without warning, she'd veer off in another direction. There was a slim chance it was a deliberate tactic, but he didn't think so.

Correction. He didn't *want* to think so. Which was even worse.

"Why wasn't I what? Going to steal your boat? I do have to get back, you know. And I do know something about boats. I helped drive those two posts in the bank to tie it up to, didn't I?"

"Right. And you know the pointy end goes first and the flat end follows. Why weren't you taught how to swim at an early age?"

She lifted her shoulders in an oddly elegant gesture and let them fall again. "I don't know. Mama said we lived too far from the pool and she didn't have time to take me, but we were probably too broke. We didn't have a lot of money. There, is that tight enough?'' She sat back on her heels and tugged his pants down over the lumpy wad of his knee.

''Perfect. Thanks.'' It occurred to him that he'd said please and thank you more in the past twenty-four hours than he had in the last ten years. Not that he was necessarily rude. It was just that in his line of work, courtesy wasn't exactly commonplace.

With Jasmine, it probably was. He knew a lot more about her than she suspected, partly from observation, partly from deduction, partly from skillfully placed questions.

She was an actress. There was a slim chance that she was also a journalist. That was a risk he hadn't anticipated. But journalist or not, the lady was by nature open, impulsive, generous and far too trusting for any woman in this day and age. She was thirty-four years old. Old enough to know better. Most women learned caution by the time they started experimenting with lipstick.

Jasmine was about as cautious as a kid with a brand-new puppy. Besides, she didn't wear lipstick.

What kind of an actress didn't wear lipstick?

One who had a face full of poison ivy? One who was stuck in the swamp without her war paint? One who wasn't interested in impressing a man with her looks?

Jeez.

At the moment, they were stuck with each other. He could've told her about the outboard he had stashed away, but he couldn't afford to let her go back and leave him in this condition. He'd be a sitting duck for anyone who came snooping around, and if that was paranoid, so be it. Paranoia went with the territory. A solid case of preventive paranoia was better than a Kevlar vest when it came to keeping a spook alive.

And Lyon fully intended to stay alive. He had one more job to do. He owed it to Giotto and McNeil. But first, he had to get himself in shape, and while he was doing that he had to go over and over the pieces of the puzzle in his possession until he came up with the missing one.

So he'd keep her here a few more days, at least until he was able to move to a new location. It wouldn't be hard to do. It seemed he'd caught himself that rarest of all creatures: a tenderhearted woman. Would she go off and leave a helpless invalid out here in the wilderness?

Hell no, she wouldn't.

Besides, her hands were in no condition to row the seven miles it would take to reach a road. Even if she got to digging around and found his cell phone, it wouldn't do her any good. The only tower within five miles in any direction was an unmanned fire tower. Even with fresh batteries, the thing was as good as dead.

"Want me to help you walk around some?"

"I'm not a cripple," he growled.

"I know that. I only meant, if you want to move around some to sort of loosen up, I'll be glad to steady you so you don't trip over a root or a vine or something. It's not like we have a sidewalk."

"Yeah. Sorry. Sure, help me up and let's circle the clearing a few times."

She was too damned softhearted. With a little encouragement, he could probably have her leading him to the bathroom. Either she was a far better actress than he'd thought—in which case he was in trouble—or she was too naive for her own good.

In which case he was also in trouble.

They walked until he'd loosened up the parts of him that needed loosening. Other parts would have to wait. Carefully, he lifted first one arm and then the other over his head, bending sideways three inches. Stretching it another cautious inch more. He was improving, but it wouldn't take much to set off the spasms again.

Gingerly, he flexed his knee. He'd been well on the way to complete rehabilitation until he'd overdone the rowing, and on top of that, been forced to spend a night in that damned boat. The combination had set him back at least a week.

He couldn't afford a single day.

The sun, still riding low in the sky, reached its winter apex and began a rapid descent over the area designated on his map as Mattamuskeet Wildlife Refuge. He hadn't explored that far west yet, but he intended to. According to his information, the Lawless tract stretched at least that far, maybe farther. Some of the original tract was in the next county. Some was probably included in the refuge. In fact, from what he'd been able to determine in the tax office, the largest part had been claimed by various state and federal programs, the choicest parcels sold off for farming or logging. What was left was undivided and either inaccessible or useless or both.

"Does it still hurt?"

"Nah. It's just stiff. Thanks, though."

He patted her hand. Patted her hand! God, when was the last time he'd patted a woman's hand?

They had circled the small clearing five times. Jasmine was afraid he might overdo it and collapse, and she didn't want to have to go through the agony of getting him back on his feet. She'd heard enough profanity the last time she'd had to help him up.

Not filth and venom, though. She appreciated that, although she could do without quite so many damns and hells.

"Shall I fix us some lunch before I leave?" And she was going to leave today, she really was. She had to.

"If you're hungry."

"I'm always hungry. Mama said it was on account of I shot up so fast, I never managed to catch up."

"What else did Mama say?" She knew he was laughing at her in that solemn, tough-guy way he had, without even cracking a smile, but it didn't bother her. If he'd been Eric her feelings would've been hurt, but Eric never laughed at her. He was far too suave.

Suave was not a term that would ever be applied to this man.

She helped him back down onto his stump, which was stool-height and conveniently placed between his tent, his two metal lockers and the fire pit. Then she rummaged around in the largest locker, the one that was unlocked, and came up with crackers, a jar of cheese spread and more warm beer. The crackers were stale, the cheese spread was the Mexican kind, with salsa, and the warm beer tasted just the way it smelled.

It was probably safer than the water, though. Better safe than a bellyache or worse.

The air was cooler than yesterday, but warm enough so that before eating, she shed her borrowed coat. Before leaving she'd have to change back to her shorts and shirt, but she was in no hurry. "Is that really your name? Lion?"

"Yep."

"Like the animal?"

"Does it matter?"

She had dragged his bedroll out into the filtered patch of sunlight, and now she dropped down on it, sitting cross-legged while she attempted to spread cheese on crackers with her bandaged hands. "Not really. I only wondered what kind of mother would name her baby after an animal."

"She could have called me Dog, I suppose. Or Goat."

"Or Bear. Maybe if she'd known you better, she might have called you that."

"Actually, it's Daniel. Lyon is a family name. Spelled with a *y*, not an *i*."

"Daniel." Jasmine handed over two crackers, stretched out her legs in her borrowed jeans and wrinkled her nose at the sight of her muddy cross-trainers.

Which started her face itching again, which made her twitch all over, trying not to scratch.

Taking a deep breath, she plunged into conversation, hoping to take her mind off her troubles, which were multiplying almost faster than she could keep up with them. "Daniel's a nice name. Strong. I can't remember any villain being named Daniel, can you? I was thinking just yesterday—" Had it only been yesterday? "—that Daniel Boone lived in North Carolina. Maybe your mama named you after him—unless it was a family name?"

"It wasn't."

"Mine wasn't, either. At least, Clancy is family, but Mama picked Jasmine out of a seed catalog she was reading when she went into labor. I used to think, what if she'd been in the vegetable section? I could've been named Spinach. Or maybe Cabbage."

"Cabbage Clancy. Has a ring to it, wouldn't you say?"

Jasmine looked up to find him smiling down at her. She'd never seen him actually smile before. A quick half grin or two, and that was it, but this was a genuine smile, with all sorts of dancing little lights sparkling from those blue eyes that looked so out of place among his irregular features.

He was not a handsome man, she told herself, not for the first time. The only reason she liked looking at him was that he was...different. Rugged. Wicked looking, actually, but in a nice way.

Well. That made about as much sense as anything else in her wacky life had made lately.

"You know, I really should be thinking about getting back." Funny how reluctant she was. Just yesterday—just this morning, in fact—she could hardly wait to get back to civilization. Maybe she'd been more stressed out than she'd realized. Maybe she needed the break.

"Any particular reason to rush off?"

She thought about it. "No, not really. I mean, I could probably afford to be gone for a few more days.

I was supposed to be gone all week, at least until after Cyn and Eric got back from…"

"Cyn and Eric?"

She wanted to tell him. Of all things, she was actually tempted to pour out all her miseries on his shoulder. The only reason she could think of for such a crazy reaction was that, first of all, she'd never told a soul about Cyn and Eric and her own broken heart, or about her grandmother and how absolutely crushed she'd been to realize that her only living relative wasn't the least bit interested in her.

Besides, everyone knew you could tell a stranger things you could never tell a friend. It was like pouring your heart out in a letter, and then burning the letter. It happened all the time in movies. Wartime confessions that were supposed to end there, but never really did. Sometimes they led to true love. If the soldier wasn't killed in battle, he might show up years later on crutches, or with a patch over one eye, and the heroine, who'd been an ambulance driver or something in the war, had been faithful to his memory and welcomed him with tears and open arms. The door would close quietly behind them, and the theme would swell, and you'd know in your heart that they would live happily ever after.

There was no sex in the old movies, but that was even better. If there was one thing she had learned since moving to L.A., it was that, where sex was concerned, imagination was a lot more satisfying than reality.

And anyway, who needed sex when you could have all sorts of nice, warm, fuzzy feelings?

She loved old movies. The world had seemed a far

safer place back in her mother's day. Which didn't even make sense, considering the fact that her father had walked out and left them when her mother didn't even have a job and Jasmine was only a child.

"Jasmine? Cyn and Eric?"

She blinked at him, noticing that he had nice ears—not too large, not too small. Just right. Ears were important on a man.

"Well, you see, my grandmother—"

"Your grandmother's named Cyn and Eric?"

"Of course not, Cyn and Eric are partly the reason I went to see my grandmother. Her name is Hattie Clancy. Cynthia Kerry is my best friend. You might know her from *Wilde's Children?* She plays Hannah? Right now she's supposed to be in a plane that crashed in New Mexico, because she's actually off honeymooning with my fiancé. At least, Eric wasn't actually my fiancé—we never got around to getting officially engaged, but…"

She sighed. When no comment was forthcoming, she peered up to see Lyon slowly shaking his head. "I talk too much, don't I?"

She did, but he said she didn't. The truth was, Lyon didn't know what to make of her. If she was genuine, she was either a total wacko, or the most innocent, guileless female left on the planet. He was beginning to believe she was genuine.

And it scared the hell out of him.

What scared him even more was that she was beginning to make sense.

"I do," she said dolefully. "I don't know what's wrong with me, I'm never like this. I'm a trained journalist, did I tell you? I know all about the what, when, where, why stuff, only sometimes when I start to tell something, I don't stop to organize it first. Telling is different from writing. Normally, I make lists for everything. In fact, I'm about the most organized woman I know.''

Considering where she was from and what she did for a living, he didn't doubt it for a minute. He could have told her that the people he hung out with were usually pretty big on lists, too. Most Wanted lists. Evidence lists. Source lists. Suspect lists.

"Yeah, well…cut yourself some slack, honey. This is hardly normal circumstances.''

To his astonishment, her eyes slowly brimmed with tears. "That's probably the sweetest thing anyone's said to me in—I don't know when.''

Ah, jeez, he didn't need this.

"Mostly, people say things they don't mean because it makes them feel good—you know, like they're being magnanimous or something? They call you d-darling, because they don't remember your name. They tell you how good you look when you really don't, and they pretend they're all sorrowful because you didn't get a part, when you know good and well they'd cut your throat to get a shot at it.''

She drew in a shuddering breath and expelled it in a long, soulful sigh. He'd noticed before how much she put into one of her sighs.

He tried to think of something comforting to say. "Well, hell, Jazzy, that's just life" was the best he could come up with. He had a feeling it didn't quite fit the bill.

"No, it's not. Life is *The Waltons*. Life is—is—''

"Not a movie. Not even a TV series. Honey, life is—"

She looked up at him with those big, trusting brown eyes overflowing with tears, the tip of her nose as red as her blistered, oozing cheek, and he lost it. Flat out, clean lost it.

He opened his arms. It hurt like the very devil, but he did it anyway, and as if he were the angel Gabriel or whoever the geezer was who was supposed to welcome poor souls through the pearly gates, and she took him up on it.

It nearly killed him. He couldn't manage to stifle a gasp when the muscles alongside his spine seized up on him, but she was blubbering too hard to hear.

"Here now, it's not all that bad. Hey, poison ivy's not fatal."

"My g-grandmother didn't know me. I wrote all those letters and sent all those cards, and I even—I even sent her a picture of me with Charles Eastwood. I only had a small role in *Winds of Hell,* but he was real nice."

Lyon didn't have a clue who Charles Eastwood was, but he could understand any man being nice to her, small role or not. He only hoped the bastard hadn't taken advantage of her trusting nature.

"Shhh, so your grandmother didn't recognize you. Maybe her eyes aren't what they used to be."

Jasmine leaned back, not all the way out of his arms, because his arms felt too good, but far enough to look him straight in the face. "I'm pretty sure she has Alzheimer's disease. I never even met her before. I wouldn't have even known about her, but Daddy turned up one day and he happened to mention her before he died.''

''Uh-huh. Want to go back and try that one over again? Who, what, when and where?''

So she drew in a deep breath and filled in the bare outline of her story, which no one had ever asked for before. Never been interested enough to ask. Eric always changed the subject when she mentioned her family, such as it was.

Lyon probably wasn't interested, either, but he was kind enough to pretend to listen, and she needed to talk to someone…she really did. They said a burden shared was a burden lightened.

Hadn't someone said that?

If not, someone should.

''I was born in a little town outside Tulsa. Daddy was a horse broker, but not a very good one. Actually, he only worked for a horse broker, but mostly, he drank. I don't remember a whole lot about him, but Mama said he was always good to her, only he'd wanted to be a big rodeo star and he wasn't. He never made it past the county fair, so he drank, and he brooded, and then one day he just up and walked out and never came back.''

''You said he told you about your grandmother.''

''That was later. He showed up one day—not that I recognized him, but he had this picture of Mama and me when I was four years old, and I recognized it because Mama had one just like it. He said who he was, and I could tell he was really sick, because his skin was yellow and he was way too thin.''

She deliberately skimmed over those last few months. Discovering how very ill he really was, and how far down he was on the list for liver transplants, even if they could have worked out the insurance mess. But before she even got started on the paperwork he died. One day he was sitting in her living room, polishing his boots—he always took real good care of his boots—and the next day he was dead. Just like that.

"Well." She went to draw back in his arms, but he held her, and as it felt so good, she let him. "Anyway, I don't want you to get the wrong idea. Mama and I got along just fine. Mama cried a lot at first, but nobody had to tiptoe and whisper anymore. I could laugh and play music as loud as I wanted to, and after a while we didn't really miss him as much as we probably should have. At least, I didn't. Maybe I should have. Maybe if I'd loved him more…"

Lyon closed his eyes and held on, partly because it felt so damn good to hold a woman for reasons other than sexual—partly because he knew it would hurt like hell to move, even enough to let her go. One thing he'd discovered—it wasn't the position he was in so much as the getting there that hurt.

"Lyon?" she whispered. "I didn't mean to bore you with all this junk. About my past, I mean. Anyway, to make a long story short, Daddy told me about Grandmama, and I wrote to this nursing home. She didn't write back, but someone on the staff did, so I kept on writing. They said she didn't write anymore, but she enjoyed getting letters, and that she especially enjoyed getting gifts, so I sent candy and hand lotion and scented dusting powder and things like that. And once a lovely bed jacket I bought on sale. Yellow, with ecru lace. I guess she liked it, I never heard."

For a long time, neither of them spoke. The pale February sun quickly lost what little warmth it offered. Neither of them even missed the heat. A woodpecker drummed on a hollow tree, then squawked and flew off. A few feet away, a muskrat crawled up onto a cypress knee, took his bearings and slid silently into the water again.

Lyon moved his hands over her back, feeling the slight knobs of her spine. He couldn't reach any lower. Maybe it was a good thing. All she'd asked of him was a hearing and a little impersonal comfort. It was all he could offer.

Unfortunately, it was no longer all he wanted to offer.

Five

Staying was too easy. Physically, Jasmine had never been more uncomfortable in her life. Well, maybe once, when she'd had that awful case of flu and stayed in bed half out of her mind for three days, too sick even to call for help. Yet here she was, cold and grungy, dreaming up one excuse after another to stay one more day with Daniel in his cold, dank Lyon's den.

Not that she really needed an excuse. She could hardly board a plane full of people with her face in such a mess, could she? They wouldn't let her on. People were afraid of catching things on planes. Something to do with the air filtration system.

Besides, she had no intention of letting Cyn or Eric see her until she was completely healed over and looking fabulous.

Make that semifabulous. No point in being unrealistic.

And besides all that, Lyon needed her. He might pretend he could get along just fine without her, but he was probably the loneliest man she'd ever met in her life.

Not that he would ever admit it. He might not even be aware of it, but she was. She recognized loneliness.

Determined not to allow him to sink into a gray funk and ignore her, because it was obvious that's what he wanted to do, she asked him the names of all the birds that came around looking for the cracker crumbs she scattered for them.

He wasn't a whole lot of help. She didn't believe for one minute that the little brown bird with the rich, sweet call was a brown-speckled snuff-dipper, but she smiled, and so did he. Almost.

She'd noticed right off that when he was teasing her, one side of his mouth twitched. His eyes would go a shade lighter and crinkle at the corners. It was worth working at—prying him out of his lion-with-a-briar-in-his-paw mood, so she gave it her best shot.

He was hurting?

Tough. She was itching. Her hair was a mess, her face was a mess, her clothes, what few she had, were a mess. He thought she was a ditz, which might have hurt her feelings, but she refused to allow him to get under her skin. Instead, she played up to his expectations.

Or down to them. "Does this place have an address?"

She got "The Look." Semivillainous male chauvinist pig.

"Yeah, it's called The Ridge."

Which was a joke, because as far as the eye could see, which wasn't really all that far, what land wasn't under water was as flat as a pancake. Flatter. Her pancakes were usually lumpy. She put all sorts of healthy junk in them. Sunflower seeds, raisins, berries...

"The Ridge. I like it." At least he'd chosen to make camp on what just might be the highest spot in the entire Eastern Dismal Swamp, and for that she was grateful, because she'd woken that morning with her teeth and every bone in her body chattering, feeling as if she'd been sleeping on a block of ice. The dampness hadn't actually soaked through; it only felt that way.

She tried not to imagine how Lyon must have felt, because he'd insisted she take both his sleeping bag and his tent. She'd argued, for all the good it had done. His body might be temporarily impaired, but there was nothing wrong with his mule-stubborn will.

Once she'd thawed out enough to move, she had tied a line between two trees, following Lyon's instructions, and spread all their bedding so the sun could soak up the dew. Next, she'd put on as many layers of his clothing as she thought he could spare while he punished himself by marching in circles around the clearing, probably doing more harm than good, but you couldn't tell the man anything. He simply tuned out anything he didn't care to hear.

Still, she could hardly go off and leave him. Her conscience wouldn't let her do that, even if she'd had a way to leave, knowing that any minute now his muscles were going to go into spasms and he'd be utterly helpless again.

Once it warmed up enough, she tried fishing with the two-foot-long rod she found behind the two metal box lockers, one of which was padlocked. Against raccoons, he'd told her. She wasn't entirely sure she believed him, but it was his business, not hers.

He told her he'd brought the fishing rod for when his back was in good enough shape to cast, and she was welcome to use it if she wanted to. He suggested using a black plastic worm, which was just fine with her. She had no intention of using a live anything.

He told her how to throw it out. A dozen times, at least. Maybe two dozen. "No, don't close your eyes. That's right, nice and easy now—over your right shoulder. Aim for that floating leaf."

There were roughly ten thousand and seventeen floating leaves. She could hardly miss. All the same, she missed and hit a bunch of bracken growing on the bank.

Still, she was rather amazed at his patience. He even congratulated her when she managed to make her first decent cast. The plastic blob landed nearly four feet out in the water this time, but if there'd ever been any fish around they were long gone, scared off, no doubt, by all her botched attempts.

Lyon came and stood behind her. "Look, if you hold it this way…" He demonstrated. Reaching one arm around her, he covered her hand with his. "Thumb right here—that's it. Now, we swing—no, not like that, like this."

The worm draped itself over a cypress branch, but neither of them noticed for a while. Jasmine did notice the solid warmth pressed against her back. She noticed the arm holding her, and the callused hand covering her own. She noticed that her breathing had gone haywire.

And she noticed that hers wasn't the only set of lungs that had suddenly forgotten how to function.

"Well..." she murmured. "I hope you didn't hurt your back again."

He assured her he hadn't, but there was something in his voice that made her think *something* was certainly hurting.

"Maybe if I went to work on those muscles, I could—"

"No way. What I mean is, no thanks."

She shrugged. It was his loss. She'd learned a lot about easing back muscles last fall when she'd stepped off a ladder in the stockroom. Stepped off the second rung thinking it was the first. The shop had been so afraid of OSHA they'd insisted on paying for her treatment.

So. It was crackers and cheese and warm beer instead of fish for lunch. Later on, seeing the way he moved—or rather, didn't move—Jasmine insisted that he lie down on his stomach and let her work on his back.

"I know what I'm doing, honestly. And the sooner you're well, the sooner I can—"

"Yeah, I know. The sooner you can leave."

She could tell he didn't want to, but he did it anyway. She spread the groundsheet in a patch of sunshine and he took his own sweet time getting down. He was tense. When she straddled his thighs so that she could work without straining her own back, he tensed up even more. What did he expect? That she'd tie his arms behind him and escape with his boat?

She really did know how to give a good back rub. Sort of...

"Not bad," he muttered about the time she'd nearly massaged her fingerprints down to the bone.

His head was turned to one side, his eyes closed, both hands flat on the ground, ready to lever him up at the first sign of...whatever.

Jasmine flexed her fingers and admired the prone form beneath her. He was wedge-shaped. Broad shoulders, long back, several interesting scars. He had narrow, muscular hips, flaring into even more muscular thighs. She inhaled deeply, exhaled in a gusty sigh, and leaned into her task again, hammering with the sides of her hands, lifting with her thumbs, soothing with her palms.

He felt warm to her touch. Her hands slowed, lingering on the small of his back. Warm and silky, and slightly damp. He smelled musky, like the earth. And spicy, like the dried leaves she'd spread to pad his groundsheet. He had nice hands. Square palms, long fingers, with blunt tips. The scattering of hair on the backs was silky and dark.

"Jazz?" he murmured sleepily.

"Hmmm?"

"What's the matter, you fallen asleep?"

Dreaming maybe, but hardly asleep. Stiffening her arms, she pressed with the heels of her hands and then lifted with her thumbs. He groaned, sighed and groaned again, all without opening his eyes.

Mercy. Maybe this hadn't been such a great idea, after all.

* * *

When the sun dropped below the treetops, she folded their bedding and felt honor bound to lie and say she'd just as soon sleep out under the stars in the makeshift bedroll tonight and let him have his tent and down-filled sleeping bag back.

He didn't even bother to argue. Just changed the subject, asking if she'd mind laying a fire to heat supper.

"Sure, but I warn you, the only fire I ever laid was in the fireplace of a house we lived in for seven months when I was about twelve or so. It was going to be a surprise for Mama. I was going to have hot dogs already cooked by the time she got home from work. Instead, I smoked up the whole house and blistered the paint on the mantel, and made such a mess she made me scrape and repaint the thing because we couldn't afford to hire it done, and she was afraid the super would pitch a fit."

"Made a mess of that, too, I'll bet."

"Drips all over the floor. I forgot to spread papers."

She smiled, and in another of those odd moments of perfect understanding, he smiled back at her. "Don't worry about my floor, just don't burn down the woods, will you?" he cautioned. "Take a handful of dry leaves, a few twigs, a few of those splits of kindling over there and three of the smallest logs on the stack. I'll tell you what to do with 'em."

Lyon was on his stump again. Jasmine thought of it as his throne. From there he reigned over his small kingdom like a royal monarch.

She'd like to think she'd done his back some good

earlier, but if he was better, he wasn't about to admit
it. He never admitted anything unless he absolutely
had to. She knew more about the exterminator who
serviced their building than she did the man she'd
actually slept with for three nights in a row.

Or if not actually with, then nearby.

After three tries, a few small, satisfying flames
crackled and flared up. Jasmine stood back and admired her handiwork until Lyon suggested she open
another can of chili and set it to heat for supper.

"I wonder if I'm too old to be a Girl Scout," she
mused, bending over his diminishing supply of
canned goods.

When he didn't reply, she glanced over her shoulder to see him staring at her backside, which, she'd
be the first to admit, must look pretty lumpy under
all the layers she was wearing.

She shivered. "It's getting colder now that the
sun's beginning to go down."

"It's February. Just hope the rain holds off."

"Don't even think rain. Anyway, there's not a
cloud in the sky." There really wasn't. Only a soft,
golden haze wisping across the sky like layers of pale
chiffon.

The chili was better warm than it was cold. She
was getting a little tired of the stuff, but there wasn't
a whole lot to choose from.

So they ate warm chili and stale crackers, Lyon on
his stump and she on the plastic groundsheet, and they
talked about this and that. Mostly, Jasmine talked.
Lyon grunted the occasional reply. Sociable he was
not, but he did thaw out enough to tell her the names
of some of the trees and a few of the geographical

features he'd seen noted on various maps in the tax office. Most of the boundaries, it seemed, were either ditches, creeks or canals.

"Little Alligator Creek doesn't sound too inviting, but then, neither does Buzzard's Point. If this place doesn't have an official name, we could call it Squatter's Ridge. There was this town in a spaghetti western I once almost had a part in called Squatter's Ridge. It wasn't really a town, only a big ranch and a water hole. The main conflict, of course, was the water hole. And the rancher's daughter."

He nodded, but didn't say anything. Jasmine had an idea he didn't see very many movies.

"Although I guess this place is more water hole than ridge. What about Squatter's Hole?"

Which was when he admitted that technically, he wasn't a squatter. The place belonged to him. He'd inherited an undivided interest in it, at least.

Jasmine gazed around with fresh perspective. In the fuzzy yellow sunset, with nothing but trees, water and vines, softened by gray-green moss and feathery stands of winter-brown bracken, it was almost beautiful. It would be a fascinating movie location.

"I never heard of anyone actually owning a swamp before. Why on earth would anyone want to? I mean, it's lovely, once you get used to it, but what good is it?"

"You want the environmentalists' spin, or the tax collector's spin?"

He came close to actually smiling. It made Jasmine's heart flop over, and she told herself it was because it meant he was feeling better. That he'd benefited from her treatment. Soon he'd be well enough so that she could go with a clear conscience.

"How about both," she said. "Did I mention I'm thinking of doing a travel piece about this area? Do I need your permission?"

He grunted, stirred his chili, and avoided a direct answer. He did that a lot. Avoided direct answers. If there was one thing Daniel Lyon was, it was private. The longer she was around him, the more he intrigued her, more because of what he didn't say than what he did. Underneath that grouchy, shaggy persona he projected, she was beginning to sense vast areas of darkness.

Hidden depths, she mused, scraping the last of her supper from the sides of her bowl. If there was one thing that could capture a woman's fancy, it was a man with hidden depths.

She fairly itched to write a description of the man and the place, and of how she'd come to be there. It would make a fabulous story. Maybe even a screenplay.

Setting her bowl aside—he had only the one bowl, which he'd insisted she use, preferring the can, himself—Jasmine leaned back on her elbows and stared up into the treetops. A hazy premise began to take shape in her mind. Not a plot precisely—not yet—but she could definitely visualize a hero who looked a lot like Lyon and a heroine who looked a lot like—

Oh, sure. A wild-haired, long-legged beanpole with a face full of poison ivy. Some heroine.

"As I said before, I inherited the place, I didn't buy it."

She opened her eyes and blinked. He'd actually volunteered some information? Well, my mercy, would wonders ever cease?

Lyon had had about all he could take of innocence in disguise. If he had to spend much more time around a woman who looked like hell, who talked a blue streak—none of it particularly riveting—and who lay sprawled out before him like a seven-veil dancing girl offering herself to the head sheikh, he just might take her up on her offer.

Great. Now she even had him thinking in terms of movies.

All that saved her was that he was pretty sure she wasn't being deliberately provocative. They both knew that in the condition he was in, he was no threat to any woman. She might think she was no threat to any man, either, dressed like a scarecrow with her face broken out in a rash. The trouble was, none of that seemed to matter. He couldn't figure it. Physically, she was a mess. Mentally, she was a mess. Yet she turned him on more than any woman had in years.

He thought about it some. Not a whole lot. It didn't add up.

Lying back on one elbow with one long leg sprawled out so that the sole of her shoe actually touched the toe of his boot, the other leg bent at the knee, she continued to gaze up at him. "You inherited it? Who from? I mean, from whom?"

"Huh? Oh, the swamp." He was sorry he'd ever mentioned it. Didn't even know why he had, because he had no intention of telling her the sorry saga of his life. It was none of her business.

The lady asked too many questions.

But then, the lady was out of her element.

Which might explain why she talked too much. It was a recognized tool of his trade. Throw a person off balance and they talked. Toss in a little fear and they talked even faster.

Grudgingly, he relented. Hell, he was still human, despite a few doubts he'd heard expressed in certain quarters. "I dunno. Some old geezer who died a long time ago. I never knew him, never even heard of him until a few weeks ago when I got this letter from a lawyer saying I was an heir."

She sat up then, elbows planted on her knees. The way she moved reminded him of something he'd seen once in Africa. He and a fellow agent had been racing north toward the Sahara when they'd spotted a herd of giraffes just about the same time the giraffes had spotted their Land Rover. The guy with him—he was dead now, killed in an ambush—had laughed and called them great, gawking, ugly beasts.

Lyon had felt more like crying. To this day it embarrassed him, the way he'd reacted to a bunch of animals galloping across the plains. He'd never told a living soul. Never would.

"That's even better," she exclaimed with that sweet, guileless smile that slashed through his guard like a few rounds of armor-piercing ammo. "That you never knew him, I mean. Then his dying wouldn't be so sad. Who was he, your grandfather?"

He shrugged, and this time it hardly hurt at all. He was getting better. "Who knows? Great, maybe even great-great. Some relative a few generations back, I guess. First I knew I even had any relatives."

He didn't know if he'd been sorry or relieved to

learn that somewhere in the world there might be a handful of cousins, however distant, who shared a few genes, some DNA and maybe even a few inherited traits. From what he'd experienced so far, family was something he'd just as soon do without.

Had done without for more than half his life. His parents had fought constantly. They'd split when he was about twelve. An only child, Lyon remembered too well lying awake in the night, hearing them argue over which one would take him. Neither one of them had wanted him, so they'd shipped him off to an uncle, who hadn't wanted him, either.

The next few years had been memorable, but not in a way he cared to remember. Two years later he'd walked out. No one had come after him, not even social services. He doubted if his uncle had even reported him missing. The school probably had, but evidently he wasn't high on anyone's priority list, so he'd stayed missing and stayed out of jail, not because he hadn't stepped over the line a time or two, but because he'd been smart enough not to get caught.

And he'd managed, through a series of breaks he sure as hell hadn't deserved, to get enough of an education so that he'd eventually become a cop. A few transfers, a few favors called in and he'd worked his way into a small, tightly organized, totally off-record arm of federal law enforcement where he'd built a reputation for being efficient and effective. A little too effective.

At least someone seemed to think so.

"I read this book once," Jasmine was saying, and he slammed the door shut on his past and pretended to listen while she talked about books she'd read, movies she'd seen and roles she'd played, just as if they were in a cozy drawing room somewhere instead of hunkered down in the mud in the middle of a swamp in February with rain on the way and a one-man pup tent between them.

Idly, he listened to the sound of her husky, Bible Belt, West Coast, diction-corrected accent, but his mind was on other things. She had skin like pale silk, at least where she wasn't covered with a rash. The skin under all those layers she was wearing—layers that would smell like her body after she left—was probably even paler. She had a redhead's skin, so fine it was almost translucent.

She bathed every morning, using creek water in the only pot he'd brought with him, and his only bar of soap. He'd figured the soap would last him at least a month as he hadn't planned on bathing every day. No point in it, a man living alone in the wilderness. But damned if he wasn't getting almost as bad as she was. It wasn't easy, either, bathing in a two-quart cook pot. Not when privacy was a problem—when you were afraid your leg was going to buckle under you and the slightest wrong move could mean another week in a damned back brace.

He'd come here to get his body back in shape and to find some answers. The information was all here, filed away in his head in no particular order. It was only a matter of fitting the pieces together. All it took was concentration.

He'd destroyed all his notes before leaving Langley. There was nothing on his computer that couldn't stand scrutiny, because he knew damned well it would be scrutinized. He was counting on it. There was no such thing as a fool-proof encryption system, at least not in the United States. In other, less regulated countries they were miles ahead in that particular technology.

"Do you happen to have a needle?"

It took all of ten seconds to react. He was getting rusty. "A needle?"

She held up her right hand, the palm pink but no longer raw. "I must have picked up a splinter from the firewood. I can't seem to grab it with my teeth."

"I've got a pair of needle-nosed pliers. Here, let me see."

It was almost too dark to see, but she came up onto her knees and held her hand up under his face. She smelled of soap, and faintly of chili. Hell of an aphrodisiac, he thought wryly.

In the end, he used his knife on her. His pliers were in the war chest with a few things he'd just as soon keep private. His knife was as good as any surgical instrument. Sterilized with a flick of his Bic, it did the job easily.

Lyon looked up at the face so close to his own and felt something crumble inside him. She was all puckered up, bracing herself against pain, all on account of a splinter no bigger than half an eyelash.

"Hey, that wasn't so bad, now was it?"

"Is it out?"

"Sure is. Probably won't even leave much of a scar."

She laughed and then caught her bottom lip between her teeth, and on an impulse that came at him like a sidewinder, he kissed the all-but invisible wound and then folded her fingers over it.

"Mama used to do that," she said, her soft, raspy voice doing things to his body he could've done without.

"I'll just bet she did." His own mama had never kissed him at all so far as he could remember. Whenever he'd come in bearing battle scars from a schoolyard brawl, she'd either blessed him out or ignored him.

She drank. So had his old man. It was one of the reasons why he didn't, other than beer. Even then, three a day was his limit. He'd always liked testing himself against limits. He usually won.

An hour after the operation, Jasmine could still feel the soft, fleeting brush of his lips on her palm. Amazing, the way something so insignificant could affect her. Like a high, fast roller coaster. Like seeing the ocean for the first time, bigger than all Oklahoma.

Like seeing her daddy again after so many years and realizing that he was desperately ill, and then realizing on the heels of that, that he was a stranger.

A little kiss in the palm of her hand. It felt bigger than that. It felt bigger than the first time she'd made love. Than any of the times she'd made love, which weren't so very many, after all. She was practical by nature, not passionate.

"Is it my imagination, or does the air feel damper than usual?" she asked a little while later, handing back the tube of toothpaste she used on her finger.

"Probably your imagination. Sure you don't want a smear of antibiotic cream on your wound before you turn in?"

She shook her head. "It'll be okay. I thought I'd head back tomorrow, anyway. I could take your boat and then find someone to tow it back to you right away, so you won't be—"

"Yeah, I know. Up the creek without a paddle."

It was a standing joke between them, the reason why she hadn't been able to leave. At least it was as standing as a joke could be after only a few days.

"You'll be all right now, won't you?"

One part of her—the decent, dutiful part—wanted him to say yes, but another part wanted him to say no.

Which was the very reason why she needed to leave.

At first she thought she was dreaming. Rain beat down on the roof, on the front walk and the driveway where her mother's old Chevy Nova was parked.

Something mumbled in her ear, and she froze.

"Whaa—?"

"Shh, go back to sleep, it's only me."

Lyon.

He was in her bed?

Not really. She was in his sleeping bag, which was a double because he liked to spread out when he slept. And he was in it with her.

He wasn't spread out now. He was curved around her backside, one arm over her waist, one leg drawn up between hers, while rain drummed down deafeningly on the flimsy canvas barrier overhead.

Six

Rain. Rain, and warmth, and the smell of earth and soap and that subtle, masculine essence that Jasmine recognized as his alone. Lyon's arm tightened around her. He murmured sleepily in her hair, but he wasn't asleep.

At least, not all of him.

He was curved around her back. Without meaning to, Jasmine pressed her hips into the heat and hardness swelling against her bottom. Her heart skipped a beat. Her lungs skipped several breaths.

"This isn't very smart," she whispered.

"Mmmm?"

"I said..." She wriggled. Just a tiny bit, because there was a lump underneath the sleeping bag. Because there was a steady drip coming off the edge of the tent and more than a hint of dampness working its way through the flap.

Because he was aroused and she was aroused, and she didn't even know the man. She certainly wasn't in love with him.

Because she couldn't help it. What she wanted to do—wanted desperately to do—was to press against him even harder—to turn in his arms and open herself, and feed this ravaging beast that was threatening to consume her from the inside out.

What on earth was happening to her? She'd never been what you might call passionate. With Eric she'd pretended, but she suspected he'd known. They'd never talked about it. They'd never talked about much of anything other than his enormous ambitions and her modest ones. Mostly, they'd talked about what he wanted, and what he was doing to get it, and what he thought his chances were.

Something warm and gentle closed over her breast. She shut her eyes tightly and cupped her shoulders to protect the sensation.

"You really shouldn't," she murmured, doing nothing at all to remove his hand.

"Yeah." His voice was early-morning gruff, his breath causing her hair to tickle her face. But he didn't remove his hand. With his thumb, he stroked gently over a peaked nipple, back and forth. With each pass, electricity streaked clean through her, setting off dangerous tremors in her belly, pooling like molten lava between her thighs.

Outside, rain beat down noisily on sodden earth, on water, on the canopy of winter-bare trees. The sound was deafening, shutting out the rest of the world. Lyons's thigh, the one wedged between her legs, shifted ever so slightly, and she thought wildly, *Oh, Lord, what if his muscles lock up? We'll never get untangled!*

He was breathing hard. So was she. Why couldn't she have been sleeping on her other side when he'd slipped in beside her? Then they'd have been lying front to front instead of front to back, and who knows what might have happened?

"Yeah," he said again, his voice as rough as the bark on that big old tree that was doing such a poor job of sheltering them.

"Yeah what?" She sounded a little like tree bark, too. She certainly didn't sound like Jasmine.

"Yeah, what you said. That this wasn't a smart move."

Funny, though, how smart it felt. As if she'd been programmed since birth to lie in this man's arms, in a tent in a wet, rainy swamp in late February, with rain beating down all around, drowning out past and future alike.

She shifted slightly and managed to turn over so that she was facing him. Not touching him—at least, not all over. Nothing was going to happen. Considering his back and his knee, not to mention her own broad streak of common sense, it couldn't.

She almost wished it could.

Wished she could have something besides a fading rash to take home with her. Something she could look back on when Lyon was only a memory and think, *Someday, with the right man, under the right circumstances, I'm going to discover what the big hoopla over sex is all about.*

She had wondered. Any woman would. Sex, money and power, otherwise known as SMP—or was it

PMS?—was what drove the world according to Cyn, who might look like an airhead, but who was a very savvy woman.

Jasmine had never been quite convinced. Money and power, perhaps, but sex? She'd never been able to understand how something as ephemeral as sex could make fools of otherwise intelligent people.

But she was beginning to understand. When Lyon held her in a certain way—touched her in a certain way—the world suddenly came alive with sound and color and all sorts of special effects. Without even trying, this grizzly, grumpy bear of a man made her *feel* more, and *want* more, than any man ever had.

Including Eric, with his suave manners, his cashmere jackets and his three-hundred-dollar loafers. And she'd been head over heels in love with Eric, hadn't she?

Had she?

"I'm going to get up now," she declared in a firm whisper. And then, in a clear voice, "Why am I whispering?"

She thought she heard him chuckle, but maybe it was a belch. His face was inches from her own, every whisker, every line, every tiny scar clearly visible, even in the gray morning light.

It occurred to her that if she could see his flaws, he could see hers. At the best of times, she had a few. At the moment, she had more than a few. If she'd had a single brain cell, she would've unzipped the flap and crawled out the minute he'd crawled in.

She waited, staring at a star-shaped scar just underneath his left eye. He didn't speak. Not so much as a murmur. A muscle in his jaw twitched once, and then he closed his eyes and sighed.

She wished she could think of something devastatingly clever to say, so that he'd think about how witty she was instead of the way she looked early in the morning, all puffy-eyed, with finger marks pressed into her cheek. The cheek that didn't have a rash.

"It's periwinkle, isn't it?" She had this thing about silence. When she was nervous, silence made her even more nervous, which is why she felt compelled to fill it with words.

He opened his eyes, looking confused. Looking wary.

"That shade of blue, I mean. Your eyes? It's unusual. I know three women who wear contacts that color, but it's rare in real life, almost as rare as turquoise. I've never seen turquoise."

Devastatingly clever? Try dumb.

Their knees were all mixed up, bumping together. His felt rough because of the hair. She'd never realized how sexy body hair could be on a man. Eric shaved what little he had. So did the other man in her life. They'd almost made love once, but he'd been allergic to the perfume she was wearing. It was hard to combine sneezing and wheezing with sexual intimacy.

"Lyon, are you allergic to—?"

It was as far as she got. His periwinkle eyes, embedded in thick, stubby black lashes and a web of squint lines, came closer and closer until she felt herself going cross-eyed, and so she did the only thing possible.

She closed her eyes and let him kiss her.

It was everything a kiss should be, and a million times more. Heat, electricity, gentleness—sort of hungry, but sleepy, too, as if they had all the time in the world instead of no time at all.

Her arm, the one that wasn't curled underneath her body, slipped around his waist. She stroked his back, her fingers lingering on the slightly puckered ridge of another scar.

He used his tongue. Not aggressively—not demanding entry, but seductively. Almost lazily, as if he had nothing better to do at the moment than explore her mouth.

Which might have been more convincing if his heart hadn't been beating so hard she could almost hear it. Plink, plank. Plunk, splat.

Plink plank?

That wasn't his heart, it was the rain slacking off. His heart was going *boom-kaboom,* like jungle drums in an old Tarzan movie.

Reluctantly sliding her mouth away, Jasmine buried her face in his throat, felt the throbbing pulse there and marveled at the physiological effect one human being could have on another. It had to mean something. Her own pulse was beating so rapidly she felt giddy, breathless.

Actually, she felt aggressive. For the first time in her entire life she was tempted to take the lead. A heady sense of power swept over her as she pictured herself easing him onto his back—gently so that he wouldn't hurt anything—and then moving over him, straddling his hips with her thighs, and settling slowly, gently...

Not slowly, gently, but fiercely!

Play the "LAS VEGAS" Game and get **3 FREE GIFTS!**

1. Pull back all 3 tabs on the card at right. Then check the claim chart to see what we have for you — 2 FREE BOOKS and a gift — ALL YOURS! ALL FREE!

2. Send back this card and you'll receive brand-new Silhouette Desire® novels. These books have a cover price of $4.25 each, but they are yours to keep absolutely free.

3. There's no catch. You're under no obligation to buy anything. We charge nothing — ZERO — for your first shipment. And you don't have to make any minimum number of purchases — not even one!

4. The fact is thousands of readers enjoy receiving books by mail from the Silhouette Reader Service™. They like the convenience of home delivery... they like getting the best new novels BEFORE they're available in stores... and they love our discount prices!

5. We hope that after receiving your free books you'll want to remain a subscriber. But the choice is yours — to continue or cancel, any time at all! So why not take us up on our invitation, with no risk of any kind. You'll be glad you did!

Yours Free!

Play the

"LAS VEGAS"

Game

```
PEEL BACK HERE ▶
PEEL BACK HERE ▶
PEEL BACK HERE ▶
```

YES! I have pulled back the 3 tabs. Please send me all the free Silhouette Desire® books and the gift for which I qualify. I understand that I am under no obligation to purchase any books, as explained on the back and opposite page.

(C-SIL-D-05/98)

326 SDL CF9X

NAME   (PLEASE PRINT CLEARLY)

ADDRESS   APT.

CITY   PROV.   POSTAL CODE

7	7	7	**GET 2 FREE BOOKS & A FREE MYSTERY GIFT!**
♣	♣	♣	**GET 2 FREE BOOKS!**
🍒	🍒	🍒	**GET 1 FREE BOOK!**
🔔	🔔	🔔	**TRY AGAIN!**

Offer limited to one per household and not valid to current Silhouette Desire® subscribers. All orders subject to approval.

PRINTED IN U.S.A.

If offer card is missing write to: Silhouette Reader Service, P.O. Box 609, Fort Erie, Ontario L2A 5X3

CDMA
Member

019561199-L2A5X3-BR01

SILHOUETTE READER SERVICE
PO BOX 609
FORT ERIE ONT
L2A 9Z9

MAIL≫POSTE
Canada Post Corporation/Société canadienne des postes
Postage paid   Port payé
if mailed in Canada   si posté au Canada

Business   Réponse
Reply   d'affaires

01956 19199   01

Merciful saints alive, Jasmine, what's come over you?

Hearing the sound of her own rasping breath, she was suddenly filled with panic. Her eyes popped open. She flapped a hand behind her and fumbled with the zipper while struggling to extricate herself from the cocoon of arms and legs and fiber-filled, weather-proof nylon.

He didn't do a thing to stop her. Didn't say a word.

Silence again. "The rain's stopped," she blurted. "I'd better—it's time to—"

"I'm sorry."

On her hands and knees, she glanced over her shoulder, wondering what *he* had to be sorry about. That they almost had?

Or that they hadn't.

"I am, too. Sorry, I mean. I hope you didn't hurt your back."

He told her in three short words what she could do with his back, and it sounded interesting, but not as interesting as a few other possibilities that occurred to her.

"Don't laugh," he said, his voice more like crunching gravel than ever.

She wasn't laughing, she was hysterical. She always did hysteria as a glassy-eyed smile.

And then, wonder of wonders, he was smiling, too.

"Yeah, well...you can probably come up with a movie that covers a situation like this if you think about it for a few minutes."

She crawled the rest of the way out, hardly a graceful exit. *Crimes of the Heart?* Sissy Spacek descending the staircase trailing that chandelier?

No, that had been funny. This was merely pathetic. "Coffee," she muttered.

"Wet wood."

"Oh." She sighed. Who needed movies? What had just happened to her hadn't even happened, not really. As a romance, it would have been perfect for one of those old Carol Burnett skits.

Outside the tent, she got to her feet. Her brittle smile fell away, leaving her feeling vulnerable and a little sad. The trouble with being an actress was that one tended to overdramatize things. Even casual sex. And it hadn't even been that. Not casual, at least. Not even sex.

Jasmine wasn't foolish enough to believe she'd fallen in love at first sight. A week ago, she'd thought she was still in love with Eric. Correction: she'd tried to convince herself she was still in love with Eric. The truth was, she'd probably never loved him, she'd only wanted to be in love, and he'd been the likeliest candidate. God, what a pathetic wimp she was.

It was that old belonging thing again. Ever since she'd heard her first happily-ever-after fairy tale she'd longed to belong to someone special. Her mother had. For a little while, at least, until her father had run out on them. After that, her mother had "belonged" to any number of men, some nice, some not so nice.

The trouble was, Jasmine hadn't belonged to anyone. Sometimes she thought that was the only reason she'd ended up in Hollywood. She was still trying to recapture the fairy tale.

So far, it hadn't happened. If there was one thing in short supply in the world of Hollywood make-believe, it was Prince Charmings. Or Princes Charming. Eric had looked like a prince, but he was too self-centered ever to share himself with anyone. He liked ambition in a woman. Jasmine's ambitions were too modest.

Peter, who was allergic to her perfume, hadn't even been a contender, but he'd been nice, and she'd thought maybe...

Well. And maybe not.

Standing outside the tent, she lifted her face to the chilly morning dampness. Feeble rays of a lemony sun slanted down through the trees. Wisps of fog trailed across the still water. Before she knew it, she was slipping back into a world of illusion, where anything could happen.

From practically under her feet, a heron croaked and flew away. She yelped, and the spell was shattered.

You want to belong to someone? Fine. Belong to yourself. Get it together, Clancy. You're the captain of your own fate. Or ship, or whatever.

Jasmine didn't know much about Daniel Lyon, but she did know he was a loner. He might need her at the moment, but he resented that need. He would quickly come to resent her, too.

And that wasn't going to happen. She would leave first. Then maybe when he thought of her—if he thought of her at all—he would miss her just a little bit.

"Jasmine? Come back inside."

"No, thanks. I've really got to think about—"

"We need to talk."

"No, we don't, I need to—"

A high-pitched whine cut through her thoughts, and

she wondered distractedly if bees swarmed in February. Just her luck. Poison ivy wasn't enough, she had to have bees. Talk about the *Perils of Pauline*.

She tugged at the waffle-weave longhandles she'd borrowed to sleep in until the placket was back in front where it belonged, trying to recall if Indiana Jones had had to deal with bees, wondering if airplanes—

Airplanes?

"Airplanes! Lyon, get out here quick, someone's coming!"

Cramming her feet into her shoes, she burst out into the clearing and scanned the sky, searching for what she'd just heard.

She had heard it, hadn't she? It hadn't been a part of some wild, science-fiction, time-travel dream. Hadn't the Wright brothers done their big gig not far from here?

"Get inside," Lyon commanded softly. She hadn't even known he was behind her.

"I was right, it is a plane! Look, here it comes again!"

"Jazzy, get back inside the tent."

"There it is! It's coming right up the creek, see?"

It was small, the single engine sounding more like a lawnmower than a real airplane. Lyon reached for her just as she pulled away and raced down to the edge of the creek, waving both arms and yelling.

There was no place for a plane to land, not even a small one. One of the reasons he'd chosen this place was that it was all but inaccessible. All the same, if the pilot spotted Jasmine, he could radio their location. A fast boat could get here in well under an hour.

The plane made a slow pass and headed south. Searching? Hard to tell. There was only one thing Lyon could think of that anyone would be searching for in this particular location.

Him.

Spooks were a close-knit bunch of loners. Trust had to be earned. Even then, it was never taken for granted. When one of them turned, no one was safe.

One of them had turned. Lyon didn't know for sure which one, but he'd narrowed it down to two men. The trouble was, one of those two was the Director of Operations himself. Lyon had a feeling he was in way over his head. Of the three men in the outfit he trusted, only one was still alive.

At least, he hoped to hell Madden was still alive.

Moving closer to the woman, he watched the plane grow smaller. How long would it take him to pull up stakes and move to a new location? Would he have time?

Would it do any good?

Sunlight shafted through the low-lying bank of clouds, glinting off her hair. Momentarily distracted, he reached out and touched a wild, corkscrew curl. It was warm. Alive. Unable to check the quick response, both physical and emotional, to all the things she was and he wasn't, he swore silently.

He was still thinking of all the reasons why he had no business getting involved when the plane banked and headed north again.

"Oh, look, it saw us!" She started down toward the bank again, waving wildly.

"Dammit, Jasmine, come back here!"

A look of surprise on her face, she turned just as

he launched himself. They landed flat in the mud, Jasmine on her back, Lyon sprawled on top of her. It took several moments before she could gulp in enough air to speak.

"What are you trying to do, kill me?"

"What are you trying to do, get me killed?" He glared at her.

Jasmine glared right back. "Who do you think they are, poachers? Ivory hunters? Get real."

There was mud on his face. He looked like one of those armed and dangerous commando-types who was always slipping through jungles with a helmet and gun and a grim look on his face.

"I told you not to signal." His voice was so taut it vibrated. Eyes that had been periwinkle blue only moments before were suddenly black, with only the tiniest rim of blue.

It dawned on her then that he was naked. Strip, stark naked.

She fought to reclaim her common sense. "Well, what did you expect me to do…pass up a chance to get back to civilization?"

"You want to go back? I'll get you back." He was growling. Her wounded Lyon—her muddy, naked, wounded Lyon was growling.

"What I *want?* Well, what do you think I want, to spend the rest of my so-called vacation out here in the jungle? You didn't give me a choice, remember?"

"No?"

"No!" At least it hadn't seemed like it at the time. She could have insisted. They both knew she'd have been well within her rights to simply take his boat and row herself back if her hands could've stood the pain, and then hire someone to tow the thing back to him.

"Jasmine?"

"What?"

"I'm cold."

No, he wasn't. He was hot. She could feel his skin burning right through the single layer of waffle-weave cotton between them, setting her on fire again. You'd think a cold, wet drizzle and even colder mud would have a dampening effect on desire, but it didn't.

It was really sort of funny, only she didn't feel much like laughing. "You'd better get some clothes on. If whoever's in that plane happens to look down here, they'll get an eyeful."

"I'm not sure I can get up."

"Let me help." She wiggled. It didn't help. Lyon was tempted to ask her to close her eyes. Damned if he wasn't embarrassed. He couldn't remember the last time he'd been embarrassed. Maybe when he was about five or so, when he'd wet his pants in a supermarket because his old man had been so steamed at having to do the marketing he'd ignored the whining kid tagging along behind him.

She had to know what was happening to him. Unless he was way off base, it was happening to her, too. Crawling into the sack with her last night had been a world-class mistake, and Lyon wasn't a man who made mistakes. In his business, mistakes could be fatal.

This one might not be fatal, but it was going to be a doozy. And he was going to make it. Lying on top of her, his bare backside in plain view of any surveillance plane passing overhead, he made what just might turn out to be the biggest mistake of his entire adult life.

He kissed her again. Kissed her hungrily, thoroughly, taking his time about it. Doing with his tongue what he intended to do with his body. Plunging, thrusting into her hot, sweet depths. Deliberately driving them both dangerously close to the edge, because there was no time to linger, to savor.

"Come on," he rasped. Dragging his mouth away, he came to his feet in a smooth, balletic movement that, if he'd allowed her time to think about it, might have made her wonder.

Overhead, the plane made another slow pass. He hoped to hell they weren't armed. If they were, he was a dead man.

They made it to the tent just as the plane came directly overhead and droned off upriver. Which meant he had a small window of opportunity. More like a porthole. Lyon couldn't believe he was doing what he was doing instead of getting the hell out while there was still time, but he was doing it, all right. With full knowledge and aforethought, as the legal types would say.

The condemned man ate a hearty meal.

She was muddy. So was he. Most of hers was on the backside of his long underwear. Most of his was on his hands and knees. Neither of them was thinking about mud. At this point, neither of them was capable of rational thought. It was a wonder steam wasn't rising from their bodies.

He hadn't come prepared, and he knew damned well she hadn't because he'd gone through her purse. He also knew it would kill him to stop now, but he had to give her one last chance to bail out. He owed her that much.

"Jasmine, listen, if you'd rather not—I mean, there are certain precautions, and I didn't come prepared to—"

"Please? Lyon, I won't hurt you. I mean—well, you know what I mean."

"I know, sweetheart. I'm okay in that respect, too, but there are other considerations."

She began to shake her head. Oh, hell, if it came to that, he could marry her.

Yeah, sure you can. Marry her and fight over the kid, the way your parents fought over you.

He had a feeling she'd be a good mother. He wasn't cut out to be a father, but at least his kid, if he had one, would know what love felt like. And he'd see that they didn't lack for anything in the way of support. Hell, he'd sign over his life insurance. Lacking anyone else, he'd named a certain charity as beneficiary.

The scent of rain and wet vegetation, of sex and soap mingled in the warm confines of the tent. Suddenly, he was trembling with need, torn with indecision, the ten percent of him that was rational fighting a losing battle with the ninety percent that wasn't.

And then she touched him. Reached out and closed her hand around him, and that was it. Head back, eyes closed, he started counting under his breath, knowing he wouldn't last past single digits.

But he'd make it good for her. As close as he was to the edge, he would do that much if it killed him.

It probably would. "Easy, easy," he cautioned, laying her down on top of the sleeping bag. Wanting to rip her clothes off, he forced himself to move slowly. Unbuttoning the union suit, he folded it back, exposing her small, coral-tipped breasts.

He'd been right about her skin. She was smoother than a rose petal, whiter than a magnolia, and so beautiful his brain had obviously turned to mush. He'd been called a lot of things in his life. Poetic was not among them.

Reaching up, she touched the scar under his right eye where he'd been caught by the butt of a sawed-off shotgun.

And then her hand drifted down over his jaw, past his throat where a pulse was throbbing out of control, to trail over his chest. When her fingertips raked across a nipple he caught his breath, hoping she wouldn't notice his obvious—his very obvious—enthusiasm.

She noticed. Her eyes widened. Lyon had long since passed the stage when boys liked to brag about such things. All the same, he wished he could turn out the lights. Wished they were somewhere else, where there was soft music and plenty of uninterrupted time.

Clean sheets and a little heat would have been nice, too.

Back, don't play tricks on me now.

He touched her. Explored. She was hot and wet and tight, and that alone nearly catapulted him over the edge. Slowly, he positioned himself and eased inside her. Eyes closed, fists knotted, he braced himself to hold out for as long as it took to bring her along with him.

It was going to be a close race. He was determined

to make it good for her, but it had been too long. Slowly, carefully, he withdrew. She clutched his shoulders and made a small sound of protest.

Slowly, carefully, he thrust again, shaken to his very depths by the avalanche of fire that threatened to consume him. Lowering his head, he tasted her lips again and then risked disaster by arching his back enough to suckle her breasts.

By then he was trembling hard with the effort to control his own need.

She was trembling, too. She was surprisingly awkward, the way she moved under him. He suspected that she hadn't had much experience, and that inflamed him still more.

He felt her tighten around him, felt the beginning of her spasms, and he went out of control. Gripping her shoulders, he drove harder, faster. She met each thrust, clutching him with her thighs. Her eyes widened on a look of dawning wonder. In a tremulous voice, she said his name. "Lyon? *Lyon?*"

He bit his lip to keep from shouting aloud as wave after tidal wave of mindless pleasure swept over him.

Never before...

Never like this—!

Seconds, or maybe centuries passed, and they collapsed together. Bearing the full weight of his body, she clung to him, refused to let him roll away. Still inside her, he could feel every beat of her heart, every hot, raw rasp of breath—feel the small aftershocks that threatened to set him off all over again.

Slowly, reluctantly, he drifted back to earth. He'd have given anything he possessed to be able to freeze time, rewind, and replay the last five minutes in *slo-o-ow* motion.

But time was the one luxury he couldn't afford. "Sweetheart, we have to go," he said.

"Too late," She smiled that slow, sweet smile of hers without even opening her eyes. "I'm already gone."

It was too late, all right. Too late for second thoughts. He glanced at his wrist and gauged the time elapsed. Too much. They'd have to hurry.

The ten percent was just beginning to override the ninety percent when his gaze fell to the vulnerable hollow at the base of her throat. Without stopping to think, he kissed the fluttering pulse there. She was damp with sweat, sweet with the scent of his own soap and Jasmine.

One last kiss, he thought, wondering if she realized that it was over. Hoping she did.

Hoping she didn't.

Hell, he didn't know what he hoped anymore. The lady had royally screwed up his mind.

Seven

The way Lyon saw it, he had two choices. He could uncover the outboard and move them farther downstream, which would only be a delaying tactic—or he could pack up just enough to get by with and move them deeper into the swamp. Another delaying tactic.

Either way, a move was imperative. If he was right about that plane, time was rapidly running out.

"Lyon? Is something wrong?"

That husky voice of hers caught him halfway across the clearing. He froze, but didn't look back. Looking back was a luxury he couldn't afford. He'd wasted enough time pulling on his pants and boots.

"Rain's stopped," he said gruffly. "Time to move camp."

"Move what?" She sounded breathless. Getting dressed in a one-man pup tent wasn't easy. Crawling out, when your legs were as long as hers were, was no cinch, either.

Dammit, Lawless, don't look back!

"You think the river's going to rise that fast?"

He bent over to unlock the chest and grabbed his back for effect. His physical condition had improved far more these past few days than he'd let on. A smart man didn't lay all his cards on the table. A smart man who wanted to survive learned how to use every advantage, and the element of surprise was always good.

Not that he thought Jasmine would, or even could, use his weakness against him, but after all these years the habit was too deeply ingrained to forget. Trust had killed many a good man.

"Lyon? Is it the rain? Are we going to be flooded out?"

"Nah, the water's not going to rise," he said gruffly. "All the same, it's time to move on. I've got a better place in mind."

He was going to shoot for the house. According to the woman in the tax office it was still standing at last report. He knew the approximate location. Even had a pretty good idea of how to get there, but if what he suspected turned out to be true, they were in for some rough going between here and there. Maybe he could leave her here to make her way back the best way she could.

No way. There was a sixty-forty chance, odds against him, that he'd been followed. What he couldn't figure out was why they hadn't come in after him right away instead of waiting a week. Unless finding someone who didn't want to be found in the middle of several thousand acres of swamp wasn't quite as easy as checking out a street address. Something he'd counted on when he'd chosen to look into old man Lawless's legacy.

If he was right, then Jasmine would be in almost as much danger as he was. They wouldn't think twice about using her to get at him and then offing her when they discovered she didn't know anything.

It wasn't going to happen.

When Lyon had first gone into law enforcement, protecting the public had been only an abstract concept. Now it didn't seem quite so abstract. Not at all abstract, in fact.

After scraping away a layer of concealing debris, he whipped the tarp off the small outboard and battery. They'd save time by taking the first leg by water. He'd done some exploring. The way was clear as far as he'd gone. Once the creek veered eastward they'd have to hide the boat and cut across country for a mile or so, but as long as they got away in the next ten minutes, they stood a good chance of—

From behind him came a soft gasp. He groaned and then he swore. "Save it for later, will you? Roll up the sleeping gear and take it down to the boat."

"Lyon, will you please tell me what's going on? I'm starting to get scared."

Oh, hell. "Nothing's going on. Nothing will go on as long as you do what I say without wasting time on questions." He made his voice flat, unemotional. There was no room in his life for emotions at the best of times. This wasn't the best of times.

He'd hurt her feelings. He was a master at intimidation when it served his purpose, and right now, it served his purpose, but he didn't feel good about it. In fact, he felt lousy.

She had that look on her face again. Leading with her chin. Mad as hell, but too stubborn to argue. Lyon unlocked his war chest, grabbed the fanny pack, the cell phone, the 9mm and a spare magazine, and strapped it on. He wouldn't need the Glock where he was going. It was good for getting through airport security, but that wasn't a problem at the moment.

Jasmine dumped all their clothes—clean and dirty—together in the middle of the sleeping bag, rolled it up and tied it, using granny knots. They might hold long enough to get them into the boat. Might not. He didn't have time now to worry about it.

Even as he checked out the battery and the out-board, he was conscious of every move she made. Long legs flashing, heels digging into the mud, she stomped back and forth, bristling with indignation and questions as she bundled up armloads of soft gear, dumping everything into the boat.

Why, he wondered fleetingly, had he never before noticed how graceful a long-legged woman could be? Maybe not all of them were. Maybe it was only the woman named Jasmine Clancy—a mahogany-haired, patchy-faced woman with a raspy voice, gentle hands and all the survival skills of a newly hatched chicken.

He watched her snatch up half a dozen cans of chili and Vienna sausage and hurl them into the boat on top of everything else. Hard, as if she was trying to hole the bottom. Moving fast, he grabbed the beer before she could throw that, too, and stowed it care-fully under the stern thwart.

She was scared—he couldn't much blame her for that—and trying hard to pretend she wasn't. He wanted to take her in his arms and tell her everything was going to be all right, but there was no time.

Besides, he was in no position to offer any guarantees.

All the same, sooner or later he was going to have a big chunk of explaining to do. He was no good at explanations. Personal ones, at any rate.

On the other side of the clearing, Jasmine clamped her jaw shut so tightly it hurt. She refused to ask another question. Refused to look at him. Refused to allow him to frighten her, because that was obviously what he was trying to do. Some men got a large charge out of scaring women. She could have sworn Lyon wasn't one of them. But then, what did she know about men?

Not much. As for what had brought on all this frantic activity, she hadn't a clue. It had started when that plane had flown over, but then they'd both forgotten about the plane.

If he was worried about what had happened back there in the tent, she could have told him he didn't have to go to such lengths to make his point. She might not know much about men, but she wasn't stupid.

Damn Daniel Lyon, anyway. Did he think she was out to entrap him? She hadn't asked for any commitment, nor did she expect it. Just because she'd been stupid enough to hop into bed with a man she'd only just met— If she'd taken time to think first, she would never have done it.

And she wasn't going to think about it now. Maybe later, when she wasn't feeling quite so frightened and confused. And, of all things, sad.

She snatched the smoke-blackened cook pot off the fire pit and hurled it into the boat on top of all the rest of his grubby old junk. The stuff looked as if it had been through the wars. The thing bounced, hit the side of the boat with a satisfying clunk, and fell overboard. Crossing her arms, she spread her feet and glared down at spreading ripples, savoring a sense of righteous indignation.

Indignation that faded almost instantly, leaving her even more tired and discouraged. Things were *not* going according to script. What had been intended as a combination family reunion and vacation, not to mention an excuse to avoid an awkward social obligation, was turning out to be one big, wretched mess.

Her mother used to tell her whenever she asked when her father was coming back, that they were better off without him. That Jasper Clancy had a rare talent for doing the wrong thing at the wrong time. The man couldn't even make a simple mistake without botching it.

Evidently, it was genetic.

"Ready? Climb aboard." The command was given softly, but there was no mistaking its dead seriousness.

"No, I'm not ready, I have to use the bathroom." She lifted her chin in defiance.

He uttered a word that was short and to the point. And then he said, "Well do it, but be damned quick about it, will you?"

Her chin lost its authority. It quivered. Her eyes

filmed over. Where was the man who had made such sweet, urgent love to her less than an hour ago? Where was the man who had turned her world upside down with a single earth-shattering experience that registered about eight-point-five on her personal Richter scale?

He was standing right here before her, that's where he was. Wearing nothing but boots and a pair of cargo pants, with a big ugly gun stuffed into his little black fanny pack and a Dirty Harry look on his face.

She took a judicious step back. "I think if it's all the same to you, I'll just…um, stay here?"

"Get in the boat, Jasmine."

"No, thanks." Her smile might not win her an Academy Award, but it was the best she could do under the circumstances.

The smile faded. She shivered. It was cold. It was February. She was trapped in a scene from *Deliverance* with an armed, half-naked madman. She felt like crying, but crying wasn't going to get her out of this mess, so she glared at him instead.

Lyon didn't have time to argue. Faced with two choices, he didn't know whether to leave her here and find some way to rescue her later, or pick her up, throw her into the boat and spend the next three weeks in traction. His back was better; it wasn't first class.

Suddenly, he tilted his head. His eyes narrowed on the spot where the creek disappeared around a brush-hung curve. "I'm afraid we just ran out of options."

He spoke calmly, as if making a casual observation about the weather. When she opened her mouth to question him he cut her off, deliberately using the kind of words he knew she hated. The kind she called the filth and venom words. Seeing her wince, he felt a momentary twinge of remorse, but it was too late for remorse. Or regrets. It was also too late for retreat. His only hope now was to scare her into following his orders without question.

"Get behind the bushes and stay there," he snapped. "Don't say a word and whatever you do, don't come out until I give the all-clear, you got that?"

Judging by sound alone, the boat was in no great hurry. A lot of horsepower pushing a heavy load, approaching slowly, probably on the lookout for hidden snags. It would be on them before he could even get his own boat cranked up. Even if he managed to get underway, a trolling motor would be no match for that kind of power.

There was no way he could disguise the fact that he was armed. His jacket was balled up in the sleeping bag. He hadn't even taken time to put on a shirt.

He knew she was still there. Hell, he'd know if she was within five miles. Talk about instincts, she'd really done a job on his. "You still here? What are you looking at?" She stood rooted in place, her big dark eyes staring at him as if he'd suddenly sprouted horns. "Go!" He clapped his hands. She jumped, and then turned and loped away, back stiff, head high, elbows pumping indignantly.

At least, with those long legs of hers, she covered ground. By the time their guest rounded the thick stand of wax myrtle that hung over the bank, she was out of sight.

Assuming his best dumb-jerk attitude, Lyon flexed

his shoulders a few times, then relaxed his stance and waited, his mind automatically registering data. The boat, about a twenty-two-footer, was built for hauling, not for speed. A workboat, she was square-ended, flat-bottomed and cheaply finished. Hardly a rich man's toy. At the moment, she was loaded with what appeared to be a bundle of twelve-foot poles, some sections of PVC and half a dozen concrete monuments.

Trojan horse, he thought while he waited for the man at the controls to make his move. Nobody welcomed strangers too freely these days, not without checking them over pretty carefully.

The stranger cut the throttle and glided in toward the shore. The two men sized each other up. Lyon filed away more data. Mid-sixties, wearing camouflage, duck and denim, all pretty well-worn. Braves cap, new. Waterproof work boots. Touch of arthritis. A heavy drinker, either that or he was fighting allergies.

The workboat nosed up behind Lyon's rental and the gentleman tossed the painter ashore. Deftly, wordlessly, Lyon caught it and flipped it around the mooring stob he'd sunk into the bank. Unless the old guy was a lot smarter than he looked, he figured he could take him without firing a shot, if he had to.

Don't let me down now, back.

Trojan horse, he reminded himself again. He'd been fooled before. The last time he'd damned near bought the farm.

There were three rules in the game he was playing.

Keep your mouth shut.

Keep your options open.

And don't forget the damned rules.

"Some rain we had last night, huh?" the stranger said by way of greeting.

"Sure was. Real frog strangler."

Frog strangler? He hoped Jasmine was listening. He was beginning to get into the part.

"Figgered it was you I spotted down here."

A tingle of adrenaline raced through him, but his good-ol'-boy grin never wavered. "Hey, was that you up there in that airplane? I thought maybe it was a crop duster. I was getting ready to take cover. Heard you guys used some rough chemicals."

"Wrong time o' year. Won't even get the 'taters in for a month. Nah, I ain't no duster, I was just up there takin' pitchers. Best time o' year to see the lay o' the land. This warm winter we had, trees didn't even shed till near 'bout Christmas. Next thing you know, they'll be leafin' out again, then it'll be too late."

If he was playing a game, he was damn good. Lyon hitched up his britches, which were sagging on account of his knife and the spare magazine stashed in his back pocket. "Care to come ashore and have a beer? Afraid I can't offer you much of anything else."

"Moving out?"

"Yep. Thought I might." If he had a straw, he'd have poked it between his teeth. While he might not be up to Jasmine's standards, he was pretty damned good. He hoped she'd cooled down enough to appreciate his performance.

"Going up to the house?"

Silent alarms went off. "The house?"

"Old Lawless place. You're him, ain't ye?"

"Lawless? I understood he was dead."

The guy stepped ashore. He couldn't weigh more than a hundred pounds, from his brand-new Braves cap to his muddy waterproof boots. If he was armed, it didn't show. Which didn't mean a damned thing except that he was good.

"Maggie down at the tax office said you was askin'. You're the second one that's showed up in less than a week. Leastwise, the other feller didn't show up in person. Had his sec'etary call my office."

"Your office?"

"You said sumpin' about a beer?"

Where the devil was the beer?

In the boat.

Lyon sauntered over to the boat, conscious of the weight of the 9mm within easy reach of his right hand.

"That there thing good for snakes?" The old coot was staring at the pack that held his gun.

"Hope so. Haven't seen any so far." Lyon hooked three bottles between the fingers of his left hand just as Jasmine stepped out from behind the swag of vines.

The stranger whipped off his cap and grinned, revealing one gold tooth, five yellow ones and a few prominent vacancies. "Well, lardy, lardy, I didn't know ye brung yer woman wi' ye."

He pronounced it *woo-mern*. Lyon hoped Jasmine wasn't one of those PC conscious ladies who got all bent out of shape if a man used the wrong designation. He could do without any more complications.

"Jazzy, this is...I didn't catch your name?"

"Folks around here call me Catfish. Name's Wilburn, though. Wilburn W. Webster, at yer service, ma'am.''

Wilburn W. Webster made himself right at home. He took the stump, leaving Lyon and Jasmine to find the driest spot available and hunker down.

Lyon's knee, while it hadn't so much as twinged in the last day or so, didn't take kindly to hunkering after its recent workout.

Remembering the workout, he cut a glance at Jasmine, taking in the way his flannel shirt hung from her shoulders, just grazing the tips of her breasts, and the way his best pair of jeans creased at her thighs when she spread her knees apart and crossed her ankles.

She was staring up at the old geezer with a look of open fascination.

Which was a decided improvement, Lyon thought wryly, over the way she'd looked at him only moments earlier.

"You're from around here, aren't you?" she asked, giving him the full force of her husky voice and her big, mahogany-colored eyes. "I'll bet you know lots of good stories."

"Well now..." Wilburn W. Webster pronounced it "Waal," and Lyon barely kept from snorting. The guy was spreading it on with a front-end loader. "I reckon I know 'bout as much as most folks, more'n some. Man in my perfession, we know where folks buries their skeletons."

Jasmine hauled out the grimy little notepad she was seldom without, wet the tip of her pencil and gazed up expectantly.

"Now you take old man Lawless—"

"Lawless?" She jotted down the name.

The storyteller nodded toward Lyon, who waited for the bones to start rattling. He'd deliberately avoided mentioning his full name, figuring that what she didn't know couldn't hurt him.

"His old man, I reckon. Few generations back, though."

"Lyon's?"

"That yer name, son? That'd come from the Arkansas branch, I reckon."

"Arkansas branch? Is that one of the creeks around here? Thank God they didn't name me after Two Buzzard Creek."

The old fellow slapped his knee and cackled. "Jest like yer great-grandpappy, ain't ye, son? Always pullin' a feller's leg. Squirrel, they called him. Name was Squire. Squire Lawless. Famous man in these parts."

Jasmine scribbled rapidly. Lyon opened another beer and handed it over. He checked the sun, glanced at his watch and thought, what the hell, I'm not going anywhere now.

Squirrel Lawless, it seemed, was a professional man. A maker of fine beverages. "They say he was the best shiner east of Wilkes County. Before my time. Before my pappy's time, near 'bout. They say he traded it for cows, pigs, horses, boats—whatever a feller had to trade. Squirrel weren't a greedy man, but he died rich, all the same. You see, back there in them days, they had 'em this here thing called pro-ee-bition. Best thing that ever happened to gentlemen in Squirrel's perfession. Got so successful he even branched out into the importin' business. Had boats running all the way up to Canada. That was cash money dealin's. Big money. Yessir, he was right famous, yer great-grandpaw. There was even talk a few years back o' putting up some kind of monument, but the church ladies didn't think it'd be fitting.''

Jasmine couldn't believe her luck. She'd give anything to have a tape recorder. Wisps of steam rose from the wet earth. Her stomach growled audibly, reminding her that it was time for lunch and she'd never had breakfast.

She could eat later. Right now she was getting material she could easily stretch into a feature piece. Maybe even a short series, depending on the way it turned out.

"What happened to him, Mr. Webster?"

"Squirrel? Died o' the lead poison, they say. Some said it come from wrongfully soldered copper tubin'—others said it come from a revenuer's gun."

Wilburn W. Webster, who invited her to call him Catfish, graciously accepted another warm beer and continued his tale of Squirrel Lawless, Lyon's distant ancestor, who evidently fathered a slew of children, one of whom built a mansion right here in the middle of the swamp.

"That'd be Laurel Lee. She married Billy Lancaster. Folks come from over near Dead Mule Pond. Billy, he was a logger. Cleared more acres than a herd o' beaver before he give it up. Made him a bunch of money, what with one thing and another. Built Laurel Lee this fancy house right on the river. Only thing is, the ground weren't none too solid, and she started sinking before she was even finished."

"Laurel Lee?" Jasmine gasped, scribbling frantically.

"Naw, not Miss Laurel. The house."

"Oh, this is wonderful," Jasmine murmured, wetting her pencil stub and covering page after page with cryptic notes.

Openly peering over her shoulder, Lyon didn't think it was all that wonderful. This was his heritage they were talking about. And while he didn't need it and sure as hell hadn't asked for it, as long as he had one, he'd just as soon it involved something more respectable than moonshining and bootlegging. The guys over at BATF would have a field day if this ever got out.

"Getting late," he drawled, easing his cramped muscles by stretching first one leg and then the other. His butt was wet, his back was tired, and it was time he either fished or cut bait, as their guest would say.

Had said, in fact. "Yessirree, old Squirrel, he built hisself a real fine empire, like they say on the TV. Young'uns scattered down as far as Arkansas, clean up to New York, all the way out to Texas. Reckon you got more kinfolk, boy, than Carter's got little liver pills."

Jasmine blinked. "Who's Carter?"

Catfish was embarked on a description of the patent medicine mogul when Lyon cut him off. "How do you know all this?"

"Waal now, like I say, a man in my perfession—"

"Which is—?"

"Surveyin'. Yessir, been a legal, registered surveyor since the year '76. Maggie down at the tax office, she's my cousin. She give me a call when old man Squirrel's chickens started comin' home to roost."

If there was a plot to the rambling tale, Lyon had long since lost it. "You mean the law finally caught up with him? But that would've been—"

"Sixty, seventy years ago by my count. No sir, what I meant was, once the town o' Columbia started talkin' about declarin' a historical district all over the place, and all them wildlife and environmental folks started lettin' loose red wolves and findin' all kinds o' endangered plants and critters, lawyers started crawlin' outta the woodwork. They set in to track down ever' one o' old Squirrel's descendants. I reckon you got one o' them letters. Maggie says she give this lawyer feller a whole list o' names. Had the devil's own time trackin' 'em down. Spent so much time bent over fam'ly Bibles an' deed books, she had to go to the chiropractor."

Lyon could sympathize. With his crossed arms resting on his knees, he gazed up at a snake shed dangling from an osprey's nest in the branches of a bare cypress tree, his mind turning over the new data. A whole list of names? All his *kinfolk?*

A week ago he didn't have any family. He was used to being on his own. He liked it that way. No complications, nobody demanding answers and explanations. The last thing he needed at this particular point in his life was a flock of shirttail cousins digging into his past.

"I think that's just about the most wonderful thing I've ever heard," Jasmine said reverently.

He scowled at her, not liking the soft glow in her eyes.

Absently, he noticed that her rash was almost gone, except for one cheek being pinker than the other.

"Oh, this will make a marvelous story. I can't thank you enough, Mr.—Catfish. May I use your name? Oh, I'd give anything for a camera and a tape recorder!"

Lyon had had enough. He got to his feet without so much as a twinge, and dusted off his hands. "Getting late," he observed. "I guess if we're going to move downstream, we'd better get started."

Jasmine didn't budge. "Who are you working for?" she asked the grizzled old surveyor.

Lyon should have been the one to ask that question if anyone asked. If the guy wasn't on the level, he'd lie. If he was genuine, then Lyon didn't particularly want to know the answer. He wasn't in the market for family connections.

"Feller by the name o' H. L. Lawless from New York. Real big shot, accordin' to Maggie. She talked to the man he sent down half a dozen times."

"And you say Daniel's branch of the family, the Lyons, are from—?"

"Waal now, the Lyons, that'd be on your grandmama's side, wouldn't it, Lawless?"

Lyon looked at the old surveyor. He looked at Jasmine.

"Lawless?" she echoed.

"Right," he growled. "Look, do you want to go check out this dump, or don't you? If we're going to find it before the sun goes down, we'd better get moving."

"Waal now, why'nt you folks jest foller me? That's where I'm a-going. This New York cousin o' yours hired me to survey him out a section, centerin' on the house. Land's never been divided. Each one o' the original descendants inherited equal shares. Three, four generations down the line, I reckon it all depends on how many young'uns they all had. The New York gent was the first to speak up for the house, but that don't mean you can't challenge. That goes on all the time, especially when you got all them wildlife folks hornin' in on things. I know plenty o' folks's that's got land that's been tied up in court for years, not doin' nobody no good 'ceptin' fer the tax man."

Lyon took a deep breath while his mind raced over his options.

The old guy was genuine. He had to be. Nobody was that good. In which case, he could gamble and stay here, or...

"Okay, let's go check out this house of ours. New York can have it, but as it's the closest I'll ever come to an ancestral mansion, we may as well look it over."

Eight

Catfish left them at the eastward bend of the creek, after telling them that there was a drainage canal a quarter of a mile farther south that would lead them directly to the house.

"Billy had it cut back in the forties to get his logs out. State keeps it open for access. All kinds of environmentalists poking around in here these days." The old man accepted two more beers after offering to share his wife's packed lunch of cold collard greens, side meat and cornmeal dumplings. They declined. Although Jasmine was a little curious about the cornmeal dumplings.

With collard greens?

Mercy.

"I'll be headed back up the creek about dark. If ye think of anything ye need, I can collect it and bring it out tomorrow. I'm jest hauling material in today. Job'll take up'ards of a week, I reckon.''

They both watched until he was out of sight. Jasmine sighed. "What an utterly fascinating man. I wonder what he was like as a young man. I wonder what his wife is like. I wonder—"

Lyon scowled and cranked up the outboard. "I wonder what the hell I'm even doing here," he muttered. He'd come close to forgetting the reason he'd signed himself out of the hospital and gone to earth.

Sam Madden was one of the few men he trusted, but not even Madden knew exactly where he was. Somewhere in North Carolina, that was all Lyon had told him. That left a hell of a lot of territory to search, if he hadn't been followed.

And it was just possible that he hadn't. That his suspicions were unfounded. That once he put together all the pieces he would discover that it had all been a fluke. A simple case of bad timing. That no one had turned. That no one was out to get him.

Occasionally, things got screwed up even in the most tightly run organizations. An innocent bystander turned up at the wrong time and the whole house of cards came tumbling down. It happened.

He'd like to think that was what had happened back at the warehouse, but all his instincts said they'd been deliberately set up. There was damned little in this life he trusted, but he trusted his instincts.

At least he had until this morning. Until that plane had flown over, and he'd tackled Jasmine and ended up taking her to bed at the worst possible time.

Not that there would ever be a good time. He wasn't in the market for anything like that. Men in his line of work couldn't afford ties. Besides, if genetics counted for anything, he'd be a lousy bargain for any woman. She deserved better. She deserved a hell of a lot better.

Suddenly, she stood up and pointed. The boat rocked wildly. Lyon grabbed the sides. "I see it!" she screeched. "There it is, right through those trees!"

"Sit down, Jazzy, before you dump us both overboard."

"But there it is, right there!" A squad of winged insects caught their scent and homed in on them. It was a sign of how excited she was that she, who abhorred all insects, ignored them.

So much for his legacy. "Look, it's just an old house, nothing to get excited about." His voice was gruff, but not stern. He hoped she appreciated the difference.

"Oh, my, it looks like something out of a Faulkner novel, doesn't it?" she breathed reverently as he cut the motor and glided toward the overgrown bank.

This had been a mistake. In less than a single day, he'd used up a year's allotment of mistakes. However, as long as they were here… "Grab that bush and hold us while I see if I can find something to tie up to."

Five minutes later they stood shoulder to shoulder and stared up at what must have once been considered a mansion. There was just enough paint left to show that it had once been white. One of the four columns had fallen out into the yard and was buried under a mound of vines. There was a single pane of glass left in one of the windows. The rest appeared to have either fallen out or been shot out. Of the four chimneys, one was left standing. The roof, what was left of it, sloped gently to the southeast.

Actually, the whole house sloped to the southeast.

"Come on, let's explore." She was like a kid at an amusement park.

Lyon caught her hand. "Let's don't."

She looked at him as if he were missing an ear or something. "But it's your heritage. How can you not want to see every inch of it? There might even be family portraits."

"Yeah, and there might be a liveried butler waiting to open the door. Jazzy, the place is a mess. Even if you could get in, the floors would be rotten. It's probably overrun with rats and snakes. There's sure to be termites," he added hopefully. Animals she liked. Bugs were another matter. He wasn't sure how to classify snakes, but he figured he'd better cover all bases.

They'd be lucky if that was all they encountered. He'd seen enough evidence outside to know that it had probably been used by generations of hunters and trappers as a sort of home away from home.

In other words, the place was a garbage dump.

She looked so woebegone that he half relented. "Okay, let's walk around it and see what we can see through the windows."

Way to go, Lawless. Take the sucker away from the kid, but give her back the stick.

They picked their way through the bushes, dodging boggy places and briars—which didn't leave much foot room. A one-story section on the back had separated from the rest of the house. Either that or it had been built that way.

Jasmine sank down onto a fallen tree trunk, shoulders slumping. Lyon settled beside her, absently rubbing his knee. "This is a waste of time," he grumbled.

"No, it isn't. At least now you know where your folks lived. The longest I've ever lived anywhere, at least since I can remember, is fourteen months. It was an apartment. We had a window box. Mama tried to grow tomatoes there, but they turned yellow and died."

"We'd better head back." He was tired. He didn't need this. He didn't need her and her Hollywood notions of decaying southern mansions, either.

"Do you remember that scene in *Gone With the Wind* where—"

"No."

"But I didn't tell you which one."

"I don't watch movies."

She looked so stricken he nearly lied and said he did, but then she'd ask questions, and he couldn't remember the last movie he'd seen. Something about aliens. The extraterrestrial kind.

"All the same, can't you just picture this place with magnolia trees and live oaks, and maybe a peacock or two strolling around the grounds?"

He sighed. "Jasmine, how old are you?" She told him. She'd told him before. "Aren't you too old to play house?"

She just stared at him, another stricken look in her big, mahogany-colored eyes. "Too old to dream, you mean? I guess not."

"Damn," he said softly. Rising too quickly, he clutched his knee, but it was all right. So was his back. It was his brain that was falling apart, and he wasn't going to get it together again as long as she was around. "Come on, we're going back. When Catfish comes through tomorrow you can leave with him and go back to la-la land where you belong."

"What will you do?"

"Go back where I belong." Sooner or later.

"Where's that?"

He nearly shrugged, but caught himself in time. "Wherever I happen to be."

He didn't belong anywhere. He wasn't a settling man.

But she was definitely a settling woman, and the last thing he wanted her to do was settle on him. He was about as stable as a mansion built on the mud.

Untying the boat, he handed her in and turned for one last look, trying to visualize an old couple standing out on the front porch, their arms spread in welcome for the return of the prodigal son. Grandson. Great-grandson.

"Ah, hell, let's go." There was nothing for him here.

Not that he'd been expecting anything.

By the time they reached camp, Catfish had already come and gone. There were three empty beer bottles lined up on the bank. Lyon collected them, along with their own trash, and dumped them into the hole he'd dug away from the camp. The water table was so high he had to fill the bottles with water before he could cover them with a shovelful of mud.

"Chili again?" Jasmine called from the makeshift pantry where he kept his canned goods.

"Your choice."

"Hmmmm. In that case, why don't we celebrate and have chili?"

"What are we celebrating?"

"I'll be leaving tomorrow. I guess you'll be glad to see me go."

If she was waiting for him to deny it, she would wait until hell froze over. Sure he wanted her to go. He wanted her gone retroactively. He'd be a damned sight better off if he'd never laid eyes on her patchwork face and her big brown eyes, her long legs and wild hair and that smile that could cut through his armor faster than an acetylene torch.

They were still sipping coffee, bitter and black, when a gold and lavender dusk gave way to darkness. A few stars managed to shine through the mist that drifted up as night air chilled the sun-warmed waters of the swamp.

The air smelled of wood smoke and something faintly spicy. In the distance he could barely make out the lights of Columbia, the nearest small town, reflected on the night mist. Lights and distances played tricks out here in the trackless swamp.

Imagination did, too.

For instance, Lyon could imagine standing, stretching, reaching for her hand and leading her silently to the tent.

Where they would silently undress each other and then silently make love.

Or maybe not so silently.

All he knew was that there was nothing to say. Whether he took her to bed again or not, nothing either of them could say would change things between them.

She was the kind of woman who needed a husband, a home and children. She was a nester. In spite of the movie thing and the writing thing, it stuck out all over her. It was there in the way her face softened when she talked about her father and her grandmother, and the places they'd lived.

Hell, he even knew where she'd been living when she'd had her first kiss. Some little town called Minco in Oklahoma.

"Getting late," he observed, his voice scratchy, even gruffer than usual.

It was barely nine o'clock.

She made a production of gathering up cans, spoons and the bowl. He handed her his cup. "Save 'em until morning."

"I might as well wash them now, I'm not really sleepy."

Neither was he. That was the trouble.

They watched the fire burn down to a few glowing coals. From the creek came the occasional splash. Something croaked. For the life of him, he couldn't say whether it was fish or fowl. Probably a frog.

She sighed. They still hadn't had the nightly argument over who would sleep where. Considering who had slept where last night—and what had happened—he didn't even want to think about it.

Which was probably why he couldn't seem to think of anything else.

"It's not going to rain. I'll sleep outside," he said.

"Don't."

"Don't what? Don't sleep?"

"Don't pretend. If you don't want to sleep with me again, just come right out and say so. I'll understand. I mean, my poison ivy and all—and I've been wearing the same clothes for three days, and they're not even mine."

He started to swear. Softly, virulently. "Dammit, do you think that makes any difference? Jasmine, grow up. You don't know anything about me. Look, you're a nice lady, but—"

"I *beg* your pardon."

"Huh? What'd I say?"

"A *nice lady?* Is that what you think I am?"

What the devil—?

"I'm a woman, Daniel Lyon Lawless. A fully grown, reasonably intelligent woman. I've been earning my own way for more than half my life, and making my own decisions, and—and—"

"And?" he prompted softly.

"I have a—a college degree."

He nearly burst out laughing at that. "So? That qualifies you to jump in the sack with any man who asks you?"

All injured dignity, she said, "If I'm not mistaken, you're the one who jumped into the sack with me. I was already there."

"I'm not talking about the first time, I'm talking about—"

"I know what you're talking about, and I don't want to talk about it. If you're worried that I might—"

He leaned forward, so close he could see her in the flickering coals reflected in her eyes. "I'm not worried about a damn thing, I just don't want you to get your hopes up. I'm not looking for any ties, and even if I were, I wouldn't look—''

"Hush. I don't want to hear any more."

Closing his eyes, he tilted his head back and wondered how he'd gotten so far off track. He'd come into the swamp with a simple mission. Sort through the details of the last job, figure out who knew what and when they knew it—and who had what to gain and what to lose by selling out.

Instead, he found himself mired up to his chin in interpersonal relationships, and if there was one thing he didn't need—one thing he had successfully managed to avoid since he was fifteen years old—it was interpersonal relationships.

"You want to go to bed?" he demanded harshly. "Fine. Take off your clothes. I've got nothing better to do."

Hearing the sharp intake of her breath, he hoped to hell his ancestors weren't hovering overhead haunting their damned swamp, listening in on his conversation. And he'd been ashamed of his great-grandpappy, the bootlegger?

The old man would've disowned him.

He'd been asleep long enough for the chill to creep into his bones when something woke him. The cold?

Sleeping cold was nothing new. He'd survived far worse conditions than this.

Quiet sobbing. Sniffles. It was coming from the tent, and he stared up into the thick darkness and waited for her to fall asleep again. He wasn't going to make another mistake. No way. The last few had damned near killed him.

"Jasmine?" he called out quietly after several minutes had passed.

Sniffle. Hiccup. "What?"

"You okay?"

"Of course I am."

"Sorry if I woke you. I just thought you might be cold."

"I'm not c-cold."

Of course she wasn't cold. She had the sleeping bag. He had two sheets of plastic and a few scraps of canvas.

"Then how come you're crying?"

"I'm not crying."

"No?"

"No. I'm—I'm allergic."

Yeah. Sure she was. Just like he was allergic. Allergic to sleeping five feet away from a woman he'd made love to, and wanted to make love to again.

Not that it was love they'd made together. Sex. That's all it had been. Simple, no-strings-attached sex.

"Want company?" he called out softly, hopefully.

Silence. He wondered if she'd shrugged her shoulders. Picturing her lying there inside his sleeping bag—his warm, soft, waterproof, wide-enough-for-two-people sleeping bag, he thought, oh, what the hell.

Tossing off his meager cover, he rose and made his way over to the tent, leaned down and called her name. "You still awake?"

He heard a muffled sound. It was all the encouragement he needed. Going down on his hands and knees, he crawled inside, where the air was at least ten degrees warmer, and dark as pitch.

"I thought we might talk a little if you're having trouble sleeping."

Jeez, would you listen to him. Lawless, give up the spook trade. You've got the makings of a first-rate con man.

He fumbled with the zipper, and when it stuck, she reached out an arm and helped work it loose. "Just talking, though," she warned.

"That's what I said, isn't it? I mean, you're leaving tomorrow. I thought there might be a few questions you wanted to ask—stuff for your article. I picked up some information from the tax office, and there's a welcome center in Columbia where you could collect a few brochures. Maybe get a phone number to call if you run into a snag."

She exhaled with a shuddering little sigh. "That's a good idea. I think I have to go through there to get to the airport, I'm not sure. I left my map back at the motel. I know I had to drive for hours to get to the nursing home."

She edged away when he slipped in beside her, but there was no way they could keep from touching. Her foot brushed his. His hand came down on her hip. The warm scent of soap and sex and Jasmine swirled around him, clouding his senses. That and the memory of what they'd done the last time they'd shared this same space, was enough to set him off.

He'd promised himself no more sex. No more mistakes. Just a little quiet conversation, a little companionship. He'd read somewhere that men living alone reverted to a primitive state and had trouble rejoining society.

Not that he intended to rejoin anything any time soon. He'd never been very social.

"I hope nobody messed with my things. Do you think they're safe? I mean, Clemmie might think I'd run out without paying my bill."

"Nah, she wouldn't think that. You left your baggage there, didn't you? And your car?"

She nodded. Her hair brushed his chin. He was already so hard he ached. He got harder.

"I don't itch anymore," she confided.

He did, only he had an idea that wasn't the kind of itch she was talking about.

"It was Clemmie who gave me the calamine lotion. She's the one who told me about the old logging road. Do you think it could've been your ancestor who built it?"

"Billy?" He eased closer, turning onto his side so that he could curve his body around hers. "Who knows? Anyhow, I doubt if he was even mine. Maybe New York can claim him. I'm from the Arkansas branch of the family."

"You're all connected."

He knew what he wanted to be connected to, and it wasn't any long-dead logger, or a New York hotshot. He slid his arm around her waist and hauled her closer, fitting curve to curve, hill to valley. This hadn't been such a great idea.

"Go to sleep, Jasmine."

"I thought you wanted to talk."

"I think you know what I want to do, and it isn't talking."

More silence. He'd promised himself not to. That is, unless she wanted it, too. If she did—well, hell—

he'd be a fool to deny himself. Two single, healthy, consenting adults. It wasn't like he'd made her any promises.

"Jaz?" he whispered.

"Mmmm…"

"Are you—comfortable?"

"Mmm-hmm."

"Is there…anything you want?"

He could almost see her smile. She had the kind of smile that could melt a glacier. He wasn't a glacier. Hard as one, but not as cold.

"Cold pizza and a peach milk shake," she murmured. He could tell by the sound of her voice she was smiling. He could almost picture it. Funny, how knowing a woman could sneak up on a man when he wasn't looking.

"Go to sleep," he growled, drawing her even closer.

You're a fool, man. No wonder you nearly got caught…your brain's shot. You're starting to think like a civilian, one of those nine-to-five, suit-and-tie, station-wagon types you always despised.

She was snoring softly long before he ever closed his eyes. His libidinous ninety percent finally subsided enough so that his rational ten percent came into play. He remembered thinking just before he fell asleep that maybe it was time he got out of the business. He'd definitely lost his edge. A man who'd lost his edge didn't last long, and for the first time in about a million years, Lyon wanted to last. Wanted to do something with his life besides cleaning up messes other people had made.

Nine

At first she thought it was a mosquito. Considering it was the dead of winter, there were a surprising number of the pesky little devils around. She hated bugs, always had, but there were some things in life she couldn't change. Life was buggy. You either accepted it and moved on, or you dissolved into a quivering mass of…whatever.

Lying there in a warm tangle of arms and legs with Lyon purring into her hair, Jasmine tried to make plans for her immediate future. Time to get back to the real world. If she left today, she could be home sometime tomorrow. She could start organizing her notes on the cross-country flight.

You will *not think about him. You do* not *love the man. You're in lust. It's a temporary, not a terminal, condition.*

Right. She would concentrate on her future. No more stockroom work. No more cattle calls or walk-ons. No more dreams splattered all over the floor like a carton of busted eggs. She would write.

And this time she would make it as a writer because this time she had something to write about. There was her grandmother, for starters. Intergenerational relationships and the effect of broken families on the elderly. Had it been done?

Probably. She would do it better.

One-night stands, the dangers of. Enforced intimacy, dangers of, etc., etc., etc.

Shut up, Clancy.

Lyon rumbled in his sleep. It wasn't really a snore, it was more like a purr. Like a big, slumberous jungle cat. When his hand moved so that his fingers brushed her nipple, instant heat pooled low in her body. Drums throbbed along her veins.

Had he done it intentionally?

No, he was still sleeping. All the same, she reached up, clasped his wrist and eased his hand back to her shoulder. Concentration wasn't easy for a woman who'd been referred to as "that flaky redhead" more times than she cared to remember.

But all that was about to change. Getting into the role, she pictured a computer screen and tried to read the words written there. Something with Jasmine and jungle. She liked alliteration.

Swamp. Not steamy tropical jungle, but dark, brooding swamp. Forget *Creature from the Black Lagoon,* think Edgar Allan Poe. Think ravens quothing "nevermore."

How many people even knew such a place existed

only a few miles off an interstate highway, right in the middle of farmland and small towns and all sorts of wildlife refuges? For diversity there was even a bombing range not too many miles away.

What effect did living in such a place have on the native population? Talking to Catfish was almost like stepping back in history. Evidently, time moved at a slower pace in parts of the country where people stayed in one area for several generations. They spoke of things that had taken place more than a hundred years ago as if they'd happened only yesterday. Something to do with the storytelling tradition. She'd taken a course in the tradition of storytelling back in her junior year. Now she had actually experienced it in the raw.

Oh, this was so exciting. She had so much material, so much research to do, she could hardly wait to get started. She would have to buy a computer. She would have to—

Lyon rolled over onto his back, carrying her with him so that she was sprawled halfway across his body.

With her face tucked into the hollow of his shoulder, she drew in a deep, intoxicating breath, savoring the essence of healthy masculinity.

Where was she? Oh, yes—she would have to get herself a computer and—

He slept in his briefs. Which meant that everywhere she touched she felt skin.

Concentrate, Clancy! You have plans to make.

There was just one small flaw in her plans. A flaw that, at the moment, was quietly purring in her left ear. A tough, lonely, sexy, enigmatic, irritating flaw named Daniel Lyon Lawless. No mere matter of three thousand miles between them was going to cure what ailed her. After knowing the man for less than a week, she was more attracted, more intrigued, and definitely more aroused than she had ever been in her life.

Which was a problem, because a lion, no matter how you spelled it, was not a domestic animal.

She should have known better. At her age, considering where she lived and the people she associated with, she should have known far more than she did about men. She wasn't naive. No woman in this day and age could afford to be.

Stupid—now that was something else. She had seen in Eric only what she'd wanted to see, blindly ignoring his flaws. They'd met at a cast party. Eric had hovered around her, even though he'd come with a client. He had taken his "client" home, and Jasmine had thought that was the end of it.

She'd been eating her yogurt and wheat germ the next morning, mentally rewriting editorials, when he'd called to ask her out. She'd been flattered. Eric was handsome. He was successful. He worked for one of the most prestigious agencies in town, and besides all that, he'd just ended an affair with Karen Lakehurst, who'd once been married to Scott Walton, who'd been nominated for best supporting actor three years in a row.

Three dates later her imagination was soaring. She'd pictured them shopping for houses, nothing too large, but nice—maybe something near a school. She'd pictured herself wearing designer originals instead of thrift-shop specials, being a presenter if not a nominee.

Forget all that, Clancy. From now on, we're thinking in terms of Pulitzers, not Oscars.

She had invested nine years in earning a degree in journalism, which was a darned sight more than she'd invested in her acting career. It was time to stop pretending and start living.

Outside the tent, the day grew steadily noisier. Raucous birdcalls ricocheted off dew-wet trees. Insects, or whatever that high-pitched sound was, continued to buzz in the distance.

"Lyon? Lyon, wake up."

No answer. Not so much as a twitch. She didn't know if he was shamming or not, she only knew that if she was going to get serious about her future, it was time to stop spinning dreams out of thin air. Things like this didn't help. Things like the feel of Lyon's arms around her, his warm breath stirring her hair, his legs tangled with hers, and his...

Well. That, too.

At least they hadn't made love again. She didn't know whether to be sorry or relieved. She did know it was time to get out of here, before he realized that he was the one with all the control. That hers had melted like a snowman in August.

Go now, and don't look back. If there was a defining cliché in her life, that was it. She tried not to, but sometimes she forgot and did it anyway. This entire episode in her life had been a looking-back thing. She'd like to think she could look back one day without feeling as if something valuable had slipped through her fingers, but it would take a while. Like maybe forever.

Another cliché came to mind. Been there, done that.

"Lyon?" She knew very well he was awake by now. His breathing was different. No faster, no slower, but more controlled.

She wondered what he was thinking. If he was thinking along the same lines she was, they were in trouble.

"Stay here for a minute, will you?" he murmured even as he lifted her arms from around his waist.

So much for a meeting of minds. "But I have to—"

"Stay here. Let me check something out first."

"Check out what?"

"Jasmine."

"All right, all right!" she whispered fiercely.

Rising to his knees, he peered through a slit in the tent flap. He grabbed a pair of jeans, tugged them up over his briefs, reached for his boots and slipped outside.

"Well...darn," she muttered.

The buzzing grew louder, like a swarm of angry bees. More irritated than frightened, she considered zipping herself inside the sleeping bag and staying there until the danger passed.

And then suddenly the buzzing ceased. A man's voice called out, "Lawless?"

It wasn't Catfish. It definitely wasn't bees.

Oh, God, Lyon was out there alone. She didn't know if he had his gun with him or not, didn't even know why he carried one in the first place.

What she did know was that Daniel Lyon Lawless was no ordinary businessman on a brief back-to-nature holiday. He was obviously on the run. Maybe hiding out. He might even be in the witness protection program.

And now they'd found him.

She had to do something, only what? She wasn't armed, wouldn't even know how to use a gun if she had one. For heaven's sake, she didn't even know how to use a fishing rod!

The old fake-gun-in-the-pocket routine. It would have to serve. She grabbed a pair of his cargo pants and the rope she'd used as a belt. Wearing only that and the long-sleeve undershirt she'd slept in, she eased the tent flaps open and peered outside.

Not a soul in sight. One cold, dead campfire, one sooty aluminum pot they'd recovered from the creek. Last night's dishes, washed and stacked on the metal box near the edge of the clearing.

She opened her mouth to call out, and then she heard them. Two male voices down by the creek, speaking quietly. Against a background of what passed for silence in the swamp, but was not really silent at all, Lyon's voice was distinctive for its gravelly sound. She couldn't make out what either man was saying.

If there was only one intruder, they were in luck. Lyon could take him, easy. With her as backup, they could take down Arnold Schwarzenegger, Chuck Norris and Don Johnson, easy.

"Jasmine, come out here."

Her jaw dropped. Her armed-and-dangerous finger faltered.

"Jazzy, come on out, your chauffeur's here."

Her chauffeur? Suspiciously, she peered around the

corner of the tent. Her first thought, when her brain came back on line, was that if she lived to be a hundred, this scene would be indelibly etched on her memory.

Shafts of pale sunlight slanted down through the high branches, sparkling on every wet surface. Misty veils drifted just above the surface of the creek, moving as if propelled by an offstage fan. Rising from the early-morning mist stood two men, one a lanky, half-grown boy in a red shirt.

And Lyon. Lyon in his last clean pair of jeans, boots flapping at his ankles, a gun rammed in his waistband.

Lyon with his hair standing on end, with a chin full of stubble, with an expression on his face that defied interpretation.

"My chauffeur?" she repeated, gawking at the grinning boy standing at the wheel of a boat that was painted a garish, glittery shade of fuchsia.

"Meet Horton. Clemmie sent him."

The boy spoke up. "Clemmie from the motel? She's my aunt. She got worried when you didn't come back, and called the sheriff. Catfish was listening on his scanner, and he called Clemmie, and she called me. You ready to ride?"

Lyon waited a full ten minutes before making up his mind. He could still hear the whine of the outboard in the distance. The kid was doing about a knot and a half, probably afraid of scraping his fancy new boat on a hidden snag.

Taking time only to secure the camp and toss a few things into the boat, he set off upstream. Not trying

to catch up, but being careful not to fall too far behind.

Why?

Hell, how did he know why? He didn't even want
to think about why.

Because he was running short on supplies, that was
why.

Because he'd stocked up for one man, for two
weeks, and then she'd come along. If it hadn't been
for her, he'd have made out just fine. Part of his early
training had included being dropped in an inaccessible mountainous part of Colorado with only his
'chute, a compass and a pocketknife. Eight days later
he'd walked out, a lot thinner, a lot tougher, having
learned that while ants were sour, mice weren't half
bad once you got past the initial revulsion.

He followed the twisting creek, his mind working
feverishly. This was twice he'd nearly been caught
off guard. He'd let himself be distracted, and that was
the one thing he couldn't afford. There were
risks...and then there were unacceptable risks.

Jasmine Clancy came under the latter heading.

Eventually, the creek widened out to encompass a
bay of sorts, complete with a rickety marina and a
four-unit motel. He spotted the kid's boat tied up at
the base of a finger pier and eased in behind it.

There were two vehicles parked outside the motel.
One was a rust-eaten 4×4 with a local license, the
other a rental. He headed for the rental parked outside
unit number three.

The door was open. Shielded from view, he listened as two women carried on a raised-voice con-

versation. The shower was running, but evidently the bathroom door wasn't shut all the way, either.

"I got a dryer. I'll have these things done up inside an hour. Want me to bring you something to eat?"

"Sure! Anything. And Clemmie—thanks."

She didn't have to sound so damned pleased to be rescued. He'd have brought her back. In a day or so. All she'd had to do was ask.

The woman called Clemmie stepped outside, lifted her eyebrows in his direction and asked, "Was you looking for me? I'll be in the office directly, just let me stick these things in the washer."

Jasmine took her time under the shower. She didn't want to think about how long it had been since she'd had a real bath. Washing in lukewarm creek water in a two-quart cook pot didn't quite do the job.

She dumped another handful of Clemmie's shampoo into the palm of her hand and applied it, working up a wonderful, coconut-scented lather. The motel didn't run to toiletries, but Clemmie didn't mind sharing. She'd said it was so rare to have a woman stay there, it was almost like having company.

Which was sweet, Jasmine thought. All the people she'd met since she'd come east were really nice. She would try to include them all in her article, which was already taking on epic proportions in her mind.

She would play the starring role, of course, with Lyon the male lead, but Clemmie and Catfish, and maybe Clemmie's nephew, Horton, would definitely be the supporting cast.

Oh, shoot. She was doing it again. Treating life as if it were a film script. As if Jasmine Clancy was no

more than a fictional heroine, part adventuress, part
saint. She'd been doing it for so long it was second
nature. First Cinderella and Snow White, and then
Nancy Drew. Somewhere along the line she had eased
into a make-believe life that had taken the place of
reality.

The reality of having a single parent who was almost never home because it took two jobs to support
them. The reality of always being the new girl at
school, of exploring tentative new friendships only to
have them cut short when they moved again. The reality of losing a mother to cancer and rediscovering
a father, only to lose him, too—and finding a grandmother who didn't even remember her own son, much
less the granddaughter she'd never known.

"Jasmine Clancy, you're a blooming basket case,"
she told the blur in the steamy mirror.

Wrapping the towel around her, she shoved open
the door, yelped and clutched the ends of the skimpy
towel together. "What are you doing here? You're
supposed to be back in the jungle."

"Swamp. I came in for supplies."

"Here? I don't even know if there's any place to
buy supplies around here, you'll have to ask Clemmie."

"I left my truck in town. How about hitching a
ride with you?"

She rolled her eyes. "Here we go again. If I drive
you back to Columbia, or wherever you left your
truck, what are you going to do with your boat? Leave
it here? How're you going to get back to your
camp?"

Instead of answering, he leaned his shoulders

against the wall, crossed one booted ankle over the other and regarded her steadily from those startling blue eyes that looked so out of place in a face carved from eroded granite. He'd combed his hair. He hadn't shaved. He didn't look like anybody's hero, yet she was as certain as she'd ever been of anything in her life that he was hers.

Or rather, that he could have been hers if things had been different. "You know, Lyon, you never did tell me anything about who you are, what line of work you're in and why you're living out in the swamp." Her tone was commendably casual. Conversational.

"Sure I did. Digging up roots, remember?"

"You didn't tell me that, Catfish did. Remember?" she added, openly mocking him.

He shrugged without even wincing, and she wondered how long since his back had bothered him. He hadn't been fooling that first day, but after that...

"You know my full name."

"No thanks to you," she reminded him.

"I don't have any permanent address. As for what I do for a living, I'm currently between jobs."

"I don't believe you."

He cocked an eyebrow. "Your prerogative. I don't lie."

She didn't argue. What good would it do? All men lied. Her father had. Eric had. Either with words or actions, or by omission, they all lied.

Lyon probably did all three. He even lied about lying. Worse, he didn't care if she knew it.

"All right, I'll drive you to wherever you left your truck, but I'm not bringing you back here to get your boat."

As if he were reasoning with a child, he said, "Once I have my truck, I can get back here under my own power."

It was the last straw. Since she'd first opened her eyes this morning, snug in Lyon's arms, to hear that irritating, high-pitched swarming-bee sound, things had moved so fast she hadn't had time to think.

Well, now she did, and suddenly it was all too much. Why was it that when she tried her very best not to screw up, she did it anyway? Even when she thought things through first, she handled everything all wrong. Everything. Her entire life!

What had made her think she could change now?

Glaring at him, she felt her eyes slowly fill and spill over. She snorted and wiped a wet cheek with the corner of the towel. The same moment she felt the draft on her damp body, she heard the sound of a door clicking shut.

Actually, it was more the sound of wood scraping against a sandy floor and the protest of rusty hinges, but the finality of it did her in. With all the grace of a tired and hungry two-year-old, she began to wail.

Two strides and she was in his arms. She'd been so sure he had left.

He held her, settling into the room's only chair and pulling her down onto his lap. Whoever thought sitting in a man's lap was romantic hadn't tried it with a woman who was almost as tall as the man. Her head was higher than his. She needed a chest to hide her face in while she cried her heart out.

Instead, tears dribbled off her chin onto his hair. He patted her awkwardly on the back, which was naked on account of the towel coming undone.

"There now, there now," he rumbled, and she wondered, choking back a bubble of laughter, if he'd ever said those two words in that same tone of voice before she'd blundered into his life.

"It's all right," she said, comforting the man who was trying to comfort her. "I've made a mess of your shirt."

"No problem, I'll send it out."

"I could ask Clemmie to throw it in with mine." She managed a watery chuckle. He eased her off his lap and somehow, they were both on the bed, with her hands still holding the towel in front of her. She shivered as a cold draft struck her naked backside. When they film the story of my life, she vowed silently, I'm going to be wearing a chiffon negligee in this scene instead of a rust-stained motel towel. And it'll be a four-star hotel instead of a four-unit motel.

"I really did come in for supplies," he said.

"I know."

His face was so close her eyes nearly crossed trying to focus, so she closed them. That business about out of sight, out of mind was a crock.

Lyon's hand smoothed the towel over her hip. "Goose bumps."

"It's cold."

"It's February."

They were talking all around the subject on both their minds. Jasmine reached back and drew a corner of the bedspread over them both. "Nearly March. That's almost spring."

"You asked what I did. I work for the federal government."

"As what? Postman? Tax collector?"

"Sort of an all-around troubleshooter, I guess."

"You were out there in the swamp shooting trouble?"

"Look, there's no need for you to know all the sordid details of my life, Jasmine." His hand was moving slowly over her back, sliding the bedspread over her naked skin, moving down over her hips.

No need. In other words, butt out. "I know that," she said sadly. "Thanks for humoring me."

His hand fisted. She could feel his muscles tense, and she wanted to warn him not to forget his back, but then he said, "Dammit, Jazzy, I'm not trying to humor you. I'm trying to explain why there's no future in this—this—"

"Right. You don't have to explain, I understand."

Lyon groaned. His arms tightened around her as if he would like nothing better than to shake her.

What he wanted to do was to make love to her until he couldn't move, and then he wanted to lie here and watch her talk, watch the expressions come and go on her face, listen to that soft, husky voice while she told him about the stray dog she had wanted to keep but hadn't asked for because they couldn't afford to feed it, and all the goldfish that had died and been buried with full honors. About books she had read and dreams she had dreamed, and all the other ordinary, day-to-day details of her life.

He wanted to make it all a part of his life, retroactively. He wanted to share her past, which seemed so full in spite of certain obvious lacks.

They'd both been products of broken families, subject to more than a few of life's sharp edges. He wanted to know why she'd turned out the way she

had—warm and impulsive, generous and open. Full
of dreams, as opposed to the way he'd turned out.
Bitter, suspicious, a man who chose a line of work
that only reinforced what he already knew about life:
that it held damned few rewards outside the satisfac-
tion of doing a job well.

And right now, he didn't even have that satisfac-
tion.

"Honey, we'd better move out."

"Honey?" she murmured. She was too close, too
warm, and entirely too accessible.

"Figure of speech. When in Rome..."

Her hands were playing games with the hair on his
chest. He could have sworn his shirt was buttoned up
when he'd come in here. Maybe he should've kept
his leather jacket on instead of leaving it in the boat.

"Jazzy, you're asking for trouble," he warned.

"I know. Usually I'm pretty sensible, but not always."

He caught her hand at the equator as it began to
explore his southern hemisphere. At the moment, his
south pole was extremely vulnerable. "You want to
get dressed and head for town?"

"Not particularly. Do you?"

He swallowed hard. Why lie, when the proof was
right there between them? "Not particularly."

The scent of arousal was thick and intoxicating.
Lyon thought briefly that what he was about to do
wasn't fair, not to either one of them. What he saw
in her eyes, what he heard in her voice, told him she
was already emotionally involved, and he couldn't afford emotional involvements. Especially not now,
when his whole career, if not his life, was on the line.

"Jazzy, are you sure you want to do this?" he rasped.

Her face lit up like a Christmas tree. "Yes. Oh, yes."

If she'd said no, he would've backed off. It wouldn't have been easy, but it probably wouldn't have killed him outright.

But she'd said yes, and suddenly he was paralyzed by a rush of unfamiliar feeling. Part tenderness, part protectiveness, part something that defied description, it was unlike anything he had ever experienced.

Luckily, it was swept away almost immediately by a feeling that was even more powerful. Trembling with conflicting needs—the throbbing need to be inside her, the aching need to make it last—he kissed her, taking his time about it. Savoring her textures, her flavors, the scent that was uniquely Jasmine.

Eventually, he lifted his head to stare down into eyes dark with passion, lips that were swollen with desire. Dimly aware of a feeling of masculine triumph in its most basic form, he kissed her again. Long and hungrily. Wondering in a brief burst of reason why he had never before considered kissing as a part of making love.

Because he'd never made love before. Sex was different.

This was different.

Great. Now that it was too late, he finally recognized the difference between having sex and making love.

Ten

Lyon's olfactory sense, like all his senses, was acute and well trained. She smelled of soap, toothpaste, coconuts and Jasmine. A hell of a combination. The last time he'd made love to her she'd smelled of insect repellent, coffee, wood smoke and Jasmine. Regardless of the blend, she was lethal.

He'd never had any trouble defending himself against feminine wiles. As for perfume, which was supposed to be some sort of aphrodisiac, he was immune to it. From the dollar-a-pint stuff to the pricey French kind. It came as something of a surprise to discover that he was vulnerable to a woman who wore no scent, no makeup, unless you considered calamine lotion a cosmetic; a woman who didn't possess a single wile and probably wouldn't know how to use one if she had it.

He wondered fleetingly if Clemmie kept a supply of condoms on hand. Once without was a gamble. Twice was asking for trouble. Jasmine wasn't the kind of woman who needed trouble of that sort, especially with a man who wasn't cut out to be a husband, much less a father.

Lyon prided himself that since the age of fifteen, when he'd faced homelessness, joblessness, and the usual battle with raging hormones, he'd done a pretty good job of staying on track. It hadn't always been easy, but he'd managed.

This time he'd been blindsided. Hadn't even had time to duck. If he had a preference in women it was for small, busty, flashy-dressing blondes who weren't looking for intellectual stimulation.

And then along came Jasmine Clancy with all her stealth weapons. Legs up to her shoulders. A face full of poison ivy. Maroon corkscrew curls. An artless way of asking questions that could pry answers from the sphinx.

As for her figure…

To put it diplomatically, she was built for speed, not endurance. No curves to speak of, other than a tush that made a man want to fit his hand over it. Something that could get him slapped, if not slapped with a lawsuit.

The woman was a walking, talking conundrum. She didn't wear a bra. Didn't need one. So how come he couldn't keep his eyes off the front of her shirt, watching to see if her nipples would peak under his gaze?

His hand slipped between them and he brushed his palm over her small breast. "I want to see you," he whispered. "The trouble is, I don't want to stop holding you long enough to look."

She stared at him mutely. The scent of arousal, escalated by body heat, mingled with the fragrance of coconut, soap and wood smoke.

Lyon groaned. And then he kissed her again while he teased the turgid peak between thumb and fingers. She gasped, shuddered, and started tugging at his shirt. Lifting first one shoulder, then the other, he shrugged out of it.

Her hands moved to his buckle and he sucked in his breath. Between them, they managed to get him out of his jeans and his briefs. He'd already shed his boots and socks. Thank God he wasn't wearing his gun. He'd have felt pretty damned foolish wearing nothing but a vacant grin and a fanny pack.

Her palms slid down his sweat-filmed torso, lingering on his own nail-hard nipples, tracing a scar on his rib cage, circling his navel and...

The last vestige of his rational ten percent shut down, and the remaining ninety percent took over, ending all possible hope of salvation. Without lifting his mouth from hers, he rearranged her so that she lay on top of him, and then had to shift again to accommodate his...

Enthusiasm.

"Oh, my," she gasped, lifting her head to stare down at him. A hectic pink flush spread over her throat and her face, adding a lambent glow to her dark eyes.

Arching his back, he captured her mouth again, engaging her tongue in a rhythmic duel that sent reciprocal fireworks streaking through his body. He cupped

her buttocks, squeezed, shaped, and then slid a finger
down to curl between her thighs. She was hot and
damp and ready. When he touched her in a certain
way, her sharp gasp and low, throaty moan nearly
sent him over the edge.

"Sweetheart, I still don't have protection. It's not
too late—"

"I don't care."

"There are other ways—"

"Please. Make it happen," she begged.

He made it happen. And then, he made it happen
again. He'd never known a woman to climax so
sweetly, so explosively. If he hadn't known better, he
might have thought she'd never before experienced
an orgasm from the wondering way she looked at
him.

Lifting her to sit astride him, Lyon positioned her
over his rigid shaft and lowered her slowly, bracing
himself to endure the exquisite torture. Determined
not to miss a single nuance of expression, he watched
her eyes widen again. He watched her lips part, her
head fall back. In the end, he had to shut his eyes. It
was too much. Sensory overload. He felt her tighten
around him and pulled her down until he could reach
her nipple with his tongue.

She quivered. He thrust once, twice, holding her in
place with both hands, and then they both went wild.
Rolling over in a tangle of limbs and bedclothes, he
rode her fiercely. Dimly, he was aware of something
knocking—someone calling her name. And then everything came together in a soaring, blazing, pulsating
climax that engulfed them both.

Eventually—a year, maybe a decade or so later—

they collapsed, wet, panting and throbbing. He could have sworn there wasn't a bone in his body.

Jasmine came reluctantly to her senses. *We can wait.* Had one of them actually spoken those words, or had she only imagined it?

Of course they couldn't have waited. This had been the last time. Whatever was between them ended here, ended now, and they both knew it.

Her face crumbled, but she didn't cry. Instead, she allowed the ache of loss to flow through her, the pain of it mingling with the tide of slowly receding rapture. Maybe in time she would forget the pain and remember only the pleasure.

Then again, maybe not.

Jasmine stepped back under the shower. Lyon was sprawled out across the bed, asleep. At least she thought he was asleep. If any man deserved his rest, he did, but with Lyon, she could never be sure. He was unlike any other man she'd ever known.

Unlike any man she would ever know in the future. Getting over him was going to be a long, painful process. She wasn't sure she could.

Wasn't even certain she wanted to. An aching heart was better than an empty one, wasn't it?

"Your turn," she said a few minutes later, fully dressed, but feeling defensive.

Without moving, he opened his incredible periwinkle blue eyes and gazed up at the ceiling. "If I'd known I'd have a shot at a shower I'd have brought along a change of clothes."

"I borrowed your clothes. If you'd like to borrow something of mine, you're welcome."

"Yeah, sure." He looked at her then, and smiled. Not a grin, but a genuine smile, one that kindled in his eyes, deepening the crow's-feet and those trenches that bracketed his mouth, that weren't really laugh lines because he never really laughed, but were irresistible, all the same.

"I'm going to call the airline and see if I can get a seat on a plane out, and then I'll see if Clemmie has my clothes dry. We can leave after that if you're ready."

"I need to make a couple of calls, myself."

"You want to go first?"

"No, thanks, I'll use mine." Land lines were easier to trace. Lyon was pretty sure he'd be long gone before anyone could track him down, but it didn't pay to take chances.

And you're not a guy who takes chances, right?

Go to hell, Lawless.

Swinging off the bed, totally at ease with his nudity, he retrieved his cell phone from the fanny pack he'd brought inside and tossed onto the dresser. He gave her a pointed look, and she edged toward the door.

"Um, maybe I'll check on my clothes first."

He nodded, already punching in a number. Madden had set up a series of relays that should be safe. He was on the point of collecting any messages when he heard the sound of clattering crockery, heard her swear.

"What?" He was at the door in a split second, his gun half drawn.

"Food. Clemmie brought a tray and left it outside the door, and I nearly stepped in it."

He frowned down at the rusty, flower-painted tray containing a thick white bowl covered with a plate, a matching cup covered with a saucer, an assortment of stainless-steel cutlery and something wrapped in a napkin that had already attracted a trail of ants.

Jasmine said slowly, "I wonder why she left it out here."

Lyon's silence spoke for him. Her gaze lifted slowly, taking in everything there was to take in. He could tell exactly when realization set in. A fiery blush stained her cheeks. "Oh my," she murmured, and then hurried away.

Lyon lifted the tray, flicked off the ants and took it inside. While he punched in a set of numbers, he unwrapped a chunk of buttered corn bread and bit in. He was starved. Still naked, needing that shower, needing even more to find out if he was still a target, and if not, why not.

At least one of his appetites had been satisfied. For the moment, at least.

It had turned cold just since morning. What had happened to the early spring weather they'd had for the past few days? Jasmine wasn't used to all these changes; she'd lived in California too long.

Clemmie didn't beat around the bush. "Is he going to be staying long?"

"No, I—that is, we'll both be leaving in an hour or so. If I need to pay extra, I can do it."

"No need. I'd have brought two trays if I'd known you had comp'ny." She gave Jasmine a piercing look. Seemingly satisfied, she went back to folding clothes. Evidently, the office served as the laundry room, too.

Jasmine sorted through the stack for her own things, then said, "If you could do my bill, I'd appreciate it. I need to call the airport in Greenville, but I've got a phone card. Don't forget to add on the cost of my laundry and the food—oh, and the calamine lotion."

"No charge for that. Face healed up real fast, didn't it? You're lucky. Some folks gets scars."

Two men came in just as Jasmine was leaving. Hunters, from the looks of them. She'd noticed them down by the pier on her way to the office, evidently admiring Horton's flashy fuchsia boat.

Lyon was in the shower. The bathroom door was open about six inches, which was as far as it would shut. His clothes were spread neatly on the chair, but his fanny pack was missing. Did the man actually wear his gun in the bathroom?

"You used all the hot water," he accused.

"Sorry. How'd you know it was me?"

"How many people use your bathroom?"

She hadn't meant that. She'd meant, how did he know Clemmie hadn't come back to collect the dishes.

But then she noticed that the medicine cabinet door was open so that the mirror reflected the door of the unit. He could see anyone who came in. A feeling of unease came over her. What did she really know about him?

Nothing.

How could she possibly be in love with a man she didn't even know?

Her brain told her she couldn't. Her heart told another story. It whispered of all the things she'd sensed underneath his gruff exterior. The loneliness, the basic integrity, the offbeat sense of humor that she'd glimpsed now and then when he'd dropped his guard. The feeling that he was searching for something just as she was, and that together, they might find it.

Oh, for goodness' sake, Clancy, when are you going to pack your bags and move back to the real world?

They headed north from the motel. He let her drive. That implied trust, didn't it? She could still remember hearing her mother complain because her father refused to allow a woman to drive him anywhere, even when he'd been drinking, which was most of the time.

"It's the long way around for you," he told her. "You could've headed south, picked up 264 and probably make better time."

"I told you I'd take you to wherever you left your truck."

"Thanks."

They might as well have been two strangers instead of a man and a woman who had been trapped together in the wilderness for days, who had slept together and made love together and talked about hopes and dreams and early childhood memories.

At least she'd talked and he'd listened.

So much for getting back to the real world. Given a choice, she'd rather go back to playing Tarzan and Jane in the Great Goopy, Buggy, Southeastern Dreary Swamp. Or whatever the place was called. On some maps it wasn't called anything. On others it was.

"The airport said if I could make it by three, I

could catch a flight out today with only four stops and three changes between here and LAX.''

He grunted.

''I don't know what happened to the weather. I guess it's a good thing the cold front waited to come through until I got back to my clothes.'' She was wearing a pair of jeans and a yellow cable-knit sweater.

This time, he didn't even bother to grunt.

He did point out the visitors' center and remind her of the material she could pick up on her way out of town. ''Hang a right here,'' he instructed.

Her stomach growled. He glanced at her then. ''Hungry?''

''Why no, I had half a can of chili just yesterday.''

''I think we'll pass a place not far from here. Pull in. We'll grab a burger.''

She was tempted to keep on going, but it probably wouldn't bother him at all, so she watched for something that looked as if it might be open and pulled into the unpaved parking area.

The place was deserted. There were four tables, three booths and a counter. The specials of the day were written on a mirror that looked as if it could have come from a Wild West saloon. She was trying to decide between the bean soup and the barbecue plate when the door opened behind them and two men entered.

The same two hunters she'd seen back at the motel.

Lyon didn't move a muscle, but she knew he saw them. By now he probably knew what brand of underwear they were wearing. Little escaped those periwinkle blue eyes of his.

"Barbe—" she started to say when he cut her off.

"Couple of coffees and a bag of chips to go."

She glared at him, hunters forgotten. "Why did you even bother if you weren't—"

"We don't want to miss our plane do we, honey?"

Something in his manner kept her from arguing. All the same, she didn't much like it and refused to pretend she did. The bearded proprietor slid two foam cups across the counter. Furious, Jasmine grabbed both. He tossed a handful of creamers, sugars, napkins and stirrers along with the chips into a bag and swept up the bills Lyon laid on the scarred surface.

Without waiting for change, Lyon took the bag and ushered her out the door, not even glancing at the two men in the third booth on the end. The door had no sooner shut behind them than she turned on him. "Would you mind telling me what that was all about?"

The grip on her elbow tightened so that, if the cups hadn't been covered, she would have sloshed scalding coffee all over her hand. She opened her mouth again, took one look at his grim face and shut it.

This time he drove. Not a word was spoken, but she could sense that something had changed drastically. And that something didn't concern her, except that she was here, involved up to her neck through no fault of her own in whatever game he was playing.

There was little traffic. It was easy to spot the navy blue sports utility vehicle when it pulled out of the parking lot behind them. They'd been headed east before. Now they were heading west.

"I thought we were going to get your truck."

"Change of plans."

"Would you mind telling me what's going on? It had something to do with those two hunters, didn't it?"

He was silent for a long time. She waited, fear battling anger as she noticed the way his gaze kept moving between the road ahead and the rearview mirror.

"You seen many hunters wearing a gold earring?"

"What?"

"Seen many hunters wearing a watch that costs at least two grand?"

"How do you know all that?"

He shot her a look that told her to wise up.

Her eyes widened. She drew in a breath that caught in her throat, and he reached out and touched her thigh in a gesture that was meant to be reassuring.

At least she thought it was. Right now, she didn't know what to think. For all she knew, she was being kidnapped.

No, she wasn't. Whatever else she didn't know about the man, she did know he'd never hurt her. Not intentionally. "They're not really hunters, are they?" she whispered.

"You got it."

"Then why were they dressed that way?"

"Protective coloration. Hunters don't exactly stand out around here, in case you hadn't noticed. This is big hunting country."

"That pair did? Stand out, I mean?"

He shrugged. She figured it out for herself. She was learning. "Their clothes were too new, right? And like you said, the jewelry. Who'd risk losing an expensive dress watch when you can buy something cheap and expendable for practically nothing?"

"Good going."

"Was that all? Was there something else that made you notice them?"

This time he took so long to answer that she felt like screaming. He might look relaxed, but he was doing almost eighty. There was no sign of white knuckles, but the grim set of his mouth didn't bode well for anyone who dared tangle with him.

"Maybe the fact that they checked out our license before they came in. Maybe the fact that they were watching us in the mirror. Maybe the fact that they just happened to turn up at the motel, and then they showed up in town. Maybe the fact that they're staying a steady quarter of a mile behind, not trying to catch up, but not dropping out of sight."

It never even occurred to her to take notes. There was a quality of unreality about this whole episode. The sun was shining. There were brash yellow flowers blooming here and there. A man was burning stumps at the edge of a newly harrowed field. Everything looked so normal.

Indiana Jones, eat your heart out.

Traffic picked up near Plymouth. Lyon reduced his speed to seven miles over the legal limit. He passed two fast-food places, pulled into a third and ordered two burgers, two coffees and two orders of fries at the drive-through window. "You need to go inside?"

She shook her head. "What about—you know?" She jerked her head toward the rear window, keeping her voice pitched just above a whisper.

"They stopped at the drive-in we just passed. They'll catch up."

"Oh, my Lord," she whispered. "What will you

do? Can't we find a police station somewhere? Can't you call somebody?''

He unfolded the road map, scanned it briefly, refolded it with mathematical precision and then pulled up to the window where he paid for their food. All without answering a single question.

"Eat. Unwrap mine and hand it to me once we get out of town, okay? Salt on my fries, but don't open my coffee yet, I don't want to get scalded.''

He glanced at her then, and added, "Please?''

Not until they were out of town, passing miles of farmland, a few tiny roadside communities and some logging traffic did he speak again. The sports-utility was still following, maintaining the same relative position.

"I'm going to take you to the airport and put you on the plane. I'll give you a number to call when you get home. I won't be on the other end, but leave a message, will you? I need to know that you're home safe.''

Eleven

Not until she was in the air did Jasmine allow herself to think about those last few hectic minutes. It was a small airport. There weren't many passengers waiting for the feeder airline. While she'd stood at the counter and showed her photo ID, assuring the ticket agent that no one had meddled with her luggage, Lyon had taken care of matters with the rental agency.

She'd probably looked like a fugitive on the run, the way she kept glancing over her shoulder, wondering about the two men who'd been following them. Wondering if they were waiting outside. Wondering what Lyon intended to do, and if he'd even thought about how he was going to get back to Columbia, or wherever it was he'd left his truck.

She'd grabbed her stamped ticket, raced across to the plate-glass windows that overlooked the parking lot, and there they were, leaning against the hood of the dusty navy blue vehicle.

By the time Lyon had appeared at her side, she'd been frantic. He'd handed her a folded receipt and steered her away from the window. "What's your gate number?"

"Gate number? Lyon, listen, they're outside waiting for us. You've got to get help! You've got to—"

"Shh, easy now. I want you to listen to me."

A voice over the loudspeaker announced the last call for her flight. "But I can't go off and leave you like this!"

"Jazzy, listen to me. You're going to get on that plane. You're going to go home, and the first thing you're going to do when you get there is call that number I gave you and leave a message telling me you've arrived. Right?" He waited for her to nod, and under the compulsion of his steady regard, she did. Gulped and nodded.

"Right. And then, in a week or so, or however long it takes to be sure that—ah—that—nothing happened. I mean, that—"

"That I'm not pregnant."

"That we're not pregnant," he said, correcting her, his eyes never once faltering. "You're to give me another call. Promise?"

"Will you be there?"

He hesitated just long enough for her to know the answer.

"Last boarding call for Flight 1332 to Atlanta," had come the tinny voice over the speaker.

Jasmine had felt the tip of her nose turn red. Her

eyes had begun to burn. Lifting her chin, she'd said, "If I were you, I'd grab a security guard and—"

"Yeah, sure. Listen, honey, you've got to go or you'll miss your flight. I'll be okay. I know what these guys are after, and it'll be just fine, believe me."

The image of his face had blurred. He'd grabbed her by the shoulders, kissed her hard and then turned her around and pushed her away. By the time she'd looked back he was gone.

On Monday morning, Jasmine was back at work tagging inventory in the stockroom at Marcelle's. At ten o'clock she took a break and called her agent, who was away from her desk. She left a message saying that she was back in town and available.

Not that she expected anything to turn up. She'd finally faced the fact that the odds against making it in the acting world were astronomical. It was time to grow up.

She borrowed a portable typewriter because she couldn't possibly afford to buy a computer yet, not even a secondhand one. She told herself it was excellent discipline. Using a typewriter instead of a computer would force her to think ahead.

In one respect, at least, she'd already thought ahead. She would do the swamp piece on spec, shooting for the high-end market. Once she sold that, it would be easier to sell the relationship piece on proposal. By the time her baby was born, she should be launched on her new career. She could move into a cheaper place, maybe fill in by writing ad copy for one of the small weeklies, and eventually, if she was lucky, get into something syndicated.

But then, one of her dreams had died. She wasn't pregnant. Which was certainly good news, because she could hardly support herself, much less a baby.

All the same, she was so disappointed she cried.

She waited three days before calling the number Lyon had given her. After waiting through a series of mysterious hums and clicks, she reached his answering service and left her message. "This is Jasmine. You can stop worrying."

It was with a vast sense of accomplishment one Sunday morning in early April that she put a new ribbon in her borrowed portable typewriter, rolled in a sheet of her best twenty-pound bond and started on her finished copy. At three that afternoon, she stopped long enough to massage her aching fingers, to admire the growing stack beside her, and to read over what she'd written.

It was good. Not to brag, but the piece was really, *really* good. Clean prose, action verbs—a smattering of carefully chosen adjectives, just enough to lend atmosphere. Two pages into her story and she could see it all over again—the muted shades of winter-bare trees, all that dark, slow-moving water. She could smell the distinctive fragrance of fertile earth, of spicy dried leaves, of mud and wood smoke and—

Lyon. Oh, blast. The trouble with reliving her brief sojourn in the primeval wilderness was that, no matter how objective she tried to be, Lyon was always there. At the very heart of it all.

He *was* the heart of it all.

She had honestly thought he would call and at least let her know he'd survived whatever it was that had been going on when he'd left her at the airport. He knew she'd been frantic. How was she supposed to forget the wretched man when she didn't even know if he was still alive?

Yes, she did, too. If he'd been killed, or even badly hurt, she would have felt it in her bones. After all, she was part Irish, and everyone knew the Irish had more than the allotted five senses.

But just on the off-chance that she'd been short-changed in the sensitivity department, she'd spent hours at the library searching the major eastern papers for some lead.

She'd found several stories about another Lawless who might be related but probably wasn't, unless he was the New York connection Catfish had mentioned.

Which was too big a coincidence. Evidently, H. L. Lawless was some fancy international hotshot who'd suddenly dropped out of sight. The stock market had dipped a couple of points on news that he'd divested himself of something or other. She hadn't bothered to read past that point, knowing that whatever else he was, the chances of Lyon's being an international tycoon were slightly below her chance of landing a lead part in a major film and going on to win an Oscar.

Thanks to pints of Wite-Out and the frequent use of her spelling dictionary, she was almost done when her buzzer sounded. "Oh, shoot. Not now, Cyn, please," she muttered, rolling a fresh sheet of paper into the machine. Cyn had called three times yesterday and twice this morning wanting to come over and talk about her honeymoon, which evidently hadn't lasted much longer than her suntan.

Jasmine's friendship with Cyn had suffered, but in

the end, she'd decided Eric wasn't worth losing a friend over. She'd known Cyn since her first week in L.A. They'd been through a lot together. They were as different as night and day, but it didn't seem to matter. On some levels they would never be able to communicate, but they'd shared a lot. Hopes, a few dreams—some disappointments.

And Eric.

Jasmine would have taken the phone off the hook, but there was always that one-in-a-million chance that Lyon would call.

Sighing heavily, she raked a hand through her hair, stretched and realized that she'd been sitting in the same hard-bottomed chair too long. If she took a break now, she could find a pillow, make herself a peanut butter sandwich and do a few stretching exercises while she listened to Cyn's latest tale of woe.

"Hi, have you had lunch?" she asked, swinging the door open. "I'm getting ready to make a peanut butter sandwich, so if…"

Lyon. Her mouth opened and closed. She blinked, tried to think of something intelligent, or even faintly coherent, to say and failed.

"Are you going to invite me inside?"

"I—oh—won't you come in?" She stood back and held the door, staring at the well-dressed, clean-shaven man who stepped past her.

He'd had a haircut. There was more gray showing than she'd remembered. He was wearing neatly creased khakis, a black T-shirt and a well-cut Harris Tweed jacket. Her gaze dropped to his narrow waist, and he held up both hands in mock surrender.

"I'm not armed."

"I didn't—I wasn't—Lyon, what are you doing here?"

"We had some unfinished business, remember? I thought it was time to wind it up."

Oh, for heaven's sake, just when she was beginning to get over him—or at least, if not to get over him, to relegate him to that portion of her mind where she stored fairy tales and all those old happily-ever-after movies.

"If you'd let me know you were in town, I would have—"

"You'd have what? Run out on me? Not answered your door? Taken your phone off the hook?"

"Don't be—" She crossed her arms in an unconscious defensive gesture. "I might have. Or I could have gotten an answering service to screen my calls."

She tried to interpret his expression, his mannerisms. The trouble was, he had no mannerisms. As for his expression, it was a cross between wary and hopeful.

She was the one who'd dared to hope. What did he have to be wary about?

Lyon moved past her into the room, automatically scanning and storing information. This was a mistake. He didn't belong here. It wasn't a high-end rental. Far from it. But there were rugs on the floor, pictures on the wall, plants on the windowsill. This wasn't just rooms; this was somebody's home.

Her home. She was wearing a pair of white tights with a flowered sweatshirt. Barefoot. No jewelry, but a pencil in her hair. And makeup. There was a smudge of white on her chin and her cheeks were as red as those crazy trees he'd seen on the way from the airport. All trunk and flowers, no leaves at all. "You look...different."

"So do you."

She hadn't sat down, nor invited him to have a seat. So they stood, scoping each other out like a pair of guard dogs thrown together for the first time.

"I was about to make myself a peanut butter sandwich. Would you like one?"

"What, no chili?"

Her eyes started to itch. The tip of her nose began to tingle. In about thirty seconds it would turn red and she'd be bawling her eyes out.

So she hit him in the chest.

"Ow! What the hell was that all about?"

"You c-c-could at least have told me you were all right," she wailed.

"I did. I am. What do you think I'm doing here?" He took her by the arm and steered her over to a white love seat. It wasn't as comfortable as it looked.

"What are you doing here?" She sniffled and he pulled out a handkerchief, wiped her eyes and told her to blow.

She did, and he noticed that there were no mascara stains, no rouge stains, no lipstick stains. She was just naturally...colorful.

Lowering himself beside her, he turned, one knee practically dragging the floor, and studied her silently while she got control of her emotions.

Some things at least didn't change. She was a mess. That incredible redhead's complexion, reflecting her emotions like a mirror. Those eyes, red-rimmed now, but every bit as big and as beautiful as he remembered.

"Are you sure?" he asked.

"Am I sure of what?"

"That we're not going to have a baby."

Her eyes widened still further. "You weren't going to have a baby, I was. At least, I hoped I was—or I thought there might be a chance. I told you that. I left a message with your service. And by the way, your service stinks. It's slower than molasses and noisy, and—and—Lyon, why did you come here?"

Oh boy. Here goes. "I had to know if I'd been wrong about something."

"Wrong about what?"

"About what I read in your eyes before you left. At the motel. At the airport. Even before that."

"I don't know what you mean."

"I think you do." He watched her intently, but didn't touch her. For now this was enough. Being close enough to reach out as soon as he saw some sign that he hadn't been wrong. "I think you know exactly why I'm here, Jaz. What's more, I think you've been expecting me. Tell me you haven't, and I'll go. Tell me you don't want me here and—"

"Lyon?"

He could almost feel the sizzle of electricity in the atmosphere. He didn't know what to say—was afraid of saying what was on his mind, so he didn't say anything; he just looked at her.

"Why don't you stop talking so much and kiss me?"

Hours later, Jasmine put the phone back on the hook and turned on a lamp in the living room. Lyon had showered, folded their clothes and made the bed.

He was surprisingly neat for a man who admitted that his home was a room and a bath, a bed, a telephone and a packing crate that held his books and computer.

"What about your acting career?" he'd asked her during the first intermission. Right after the standard missionary thing, just before the...well, whatever.

"I'm a writer, not an actress. I've given Hollywood every opportunity to discover me, and they didn't. Their loss is the publishing world's gain."

He came into her minuscule kitchen and wrapped his arms around her from behind. She tipped her head back onto his shoulder. "Do you want scrambled eggs or an avocado omelette?"

"Surprise me."

She had already surprised him. Even now that it was all settled, she didn't know where she'd ever found the courage to propose.

They'd been lying in her bed, not a stitch of clothes between them. The stash of condoms was still on her bedside table, untouched, right where he'd left them.

So she'd asked him and before she could even finish telling him all the reasons she thought he needed her, he'd said yes. "Hell yes," and "Yes, sweetheart," and "Right now, today, before you change your mind."

As if she ever would.

"Do you know, I still don't know exactly what it is you do. I know you're some kind of government worker, but that's all. Does that mean we have to live in Washington? I mean, I can write anywhere, but there's probably a lot of pavement in Washington, and I sort of liked living in the woods."

"How about Virginia? You haven't seen swamps

until you see the main body of the Great Dismal. Not that I've ever seen it, but we could check it out together.''

"Back up. All the way to question one. What do you do? You're not a politician, are you? I'm not going to have to go to fund-raisers and rallies and things like that?''

"God, I hope not. How about living somewhere in the country, spending as much or as little time as you want to with your writing, getting away on weekends, maybe in a few years going to a few Little League games? Omelette, if that's all right."

"What omelette?" she cried, laughing. "Lyon, you're as disorganized as I am, do you know that? Mine comes with a disorganized mind, but yours—'' She broke off and shook her head. "I'm doing it again, aren't I? Would you mind answering my first question? Are you a mailman, a bureaucrat, or what?''

Dragging a chair out from the tiny table, he straddled it, crossed his arms over the back and watched her move around the kitchen, which was all of seven square feet. "I guess I fall under the heading of bureaucrat. I'm new at it. The desk part, that is. The kind of work I was doing before—what can I tell you? I was in a line of work where we're not allowed to talk about our successes, but the press sure as hell likes to talk about our failures. Which aren't as frequent as they'd like you to believe."

"And those two men who followed us?''

"Business associates."

The unofficial type. There was a lot of gray involved in the counterintelligence world. Those two were a paler shade of gray than some he'd been forced to do business with. They'd been helpful in winding things up. For a price.

An egg in each hand, Jasmine dropped into the opposite chair and stared at him. "Are you saying you're some kind of an—an undercover operator? A spy?"

He laughed at that. "I wouldn't call it that, exactly. Let's just say that what I was doing before entailed things I won't be doing in the future. As a matter of fact, I just got a promotion."

Yeah, sure he had. His D.O. was about to be indicted. Both he and Madden would have to testify at the hearing, which wasn't going to be pleasant, but he'd do it. It was part of the job.

Once he took over as the new assistant Director of Operations, he'd be in a position to help sort through the wreckage and rebuild something that would function effectively in the post-cold-war world.

And while he was at it, he would build himself something that would make all those bleak years worthwhile. A life. A home, a family—something to serve as an anchor.

"Lyon, tell me again," she whispered when his silence lasted a few beats too long.

His face crinkled in a smile. He'd smiled more with her in a few hours than he had in the past twenty years.

"What, that I love you? That's old news. That you're going to be the mother of my son and win a Pulitzer Prize for literature and learn how to fish and darn socks and operate a riding lawnmower and maybe even learn to like warm beer?"

"Don't push it, Lawless. How about two out of three?"

"How about three out of six, my choice?"

"You're on."

* * * * *

Take 4 bestselling love stories FREE

Plus get a FREE surprise gift!

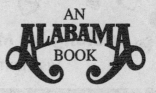

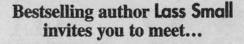